THE DEMON OF MILLER'S CROSSING

David Clark

CONTENTS

1 4
2 8
3 13
4 16
5 20
6 24
7 27
8 29
9 34
10 39
11 44
12 49
13 54
14 57
15 62
16 68
17 71
18 73
19 79
20 80
21 85
22 88
23 90
24 95
25 99
26 103
27 107
28 111
29 115
30 119

1..124
Also by David Clark...129
What Did You Think of THe DeMON of MILLER'S CROSSING?..............................132
About the Author...133

1

"What are you guys doing back in this dark corner, huh?", Sarah asked the two flickering figures in the back of old man Tyson's barn. He saw them run in there just before sunset and immediately called for help. There had been problems on his property for the last several days. The chickens were spooked and his cows were so upset they wouldn't produce any milk, and his wife went on and on about not feeling right. At first, he blew it off as his wife just being her odd self, but the chickens and cows were something different. If they weren't acting right, then something was wrong. He caught a glimpse of something running through his farm the night before, but he thought it had left. Today it was back, and it had a friend.

The two flickering vapors paid no attention to her as she inched closer. She held her hand out as if trying to lure a leery puppy out from under the bed with a treat. Inch by inch, she moved closer. With each step she ignored the chill that ran up her spine, and the cold sweat that gathered on the back of her neck. Those were feelings she felt almost every day and was used to them by now. The dark pit she felt in her stomach was a less frequent sensation, but unfortunately it had become more common than it should. She felt the evil within these things and knew just how dangerous they could be. Her first experience was with another very dangerous demon. These two were far weaker than that one, but her training taught her you never let your guard down, any of these entities can be deadly to her, and everyone around.

"Come on. Can I show you what I have in my hand?", she asked, holding her right hand out further. Both entities were still ignoring her presence, or were they? One glanced in her general direction a few times, with the beady black orbs he had for eyes. They felt it, and she knew it. They always felt it, and the closer they were to it, the feeling, the fear, became stronger.

The barn door behind her opened with a loud creak and squeal of the rusty metal wheel and hinge. Sarah looked back at the door, as did both entities. Father Murray poked his head through the door and asked, "Sarah," he stopped and coughed twice, "do you need any-".

Both entities screeched and howled as they turned and rushed toward the door.

"God dammit!", Sarah exclaimed. She opened her palm, exposing the old wooden cross hidden in it. As the entities reached her, she swung it out at the end of a cord she had looped around it and exclaimed, "Be gone, foul beast. You are not the image of God and not permitted in his realm." The cross contacted one, sending the creature away in a cloud of vapor. She pulled the rope in just as the second entity took a swipe at her. A quick duck and forward roll kept her from being hit. The creature moved past her and headed to the door. She pulled the cross into her hand and then threw her own punch, connecting with the side of the great beast. Flames burst from its side, and it fell to the ground in pain. It screamed and howled with a sound that raped the silence of the night air.

Sarah circled around it. The cross was in her right hand and extended toward the beast at all times. "You need to go, too. Go follow your friend to the bowels of hell. Never to return to this realm." Her voice was forceful, not a tad of fear in it, as her left hand retrieved a small vial of water from her pocket. With her thumb she flipped the top off and splashed it on the beast in the shape of a cross. The water froze on contact with the beast. "With this, I seal your fate. You are banished from this world, never to return."

The creature shuddered and moaned on the floor. The flickering sped up until it was not there, more than it was. Eventually, it disappeared altogether, with just a layer of red fog where it had originally laid. The fog soon dissipated, and Sarah walked toward the door.

"I said I had it," she said as she passed Father Murray standing at the door.

Father Murray wiped his nose with the red paisley handkerchief he had tucked tightly in his left hand. He pulled his collar up to guard against the damp night air and followed Sarah. "Oh, I know," he said. "Just was there in case you needed some help."

"I don't need any help. As you saw, I had it under control until you antagonized them."

"Well.. um.. yeah..," responded Father Murray. "Why did you banish him for all eternity? You can't use that kind of prayer haphazardly. We still don't know enough about the afterlife. Maybe we are reincarnated, and that poor soul will never be allowed back."

Sarah kept walking, now ten feet in front of Father Murray. "Nothing to worry about there. Neither of them were human. Even you should have been able to see that. They were not one of God's creatures. At least not ones he planned for this world."

Father Murray struggled to keep up with her pace as she trounced through the high grass, out toward the driveway and her car. The severe cold he had didn't make things any easier. "Sarah, you can't play God," he pointed out. "Some of those decisions are not yours to make."

Sarah stopped and spun around, startling the old priest. "You are the wrong person to lecture me about playing God. Those two were one of your doings. Not ones I released. I can feel how long they have been in this world, and those had been here a while." Her words were harsh, but her tone was harsher, which she realized and stopped to wait for him. Father Murray was a well-meaning family friend, and they both shared a bond, which some might consider a scar or branding. "Look, we both have enough blood on our hands from our mistakes. I am committed to fixing mine." She threw an arm around the old priest's shoulder's and said, "Now, let's get you out of here before the night air makes a ghost out of you. I don't want to have to send you out of here."

Sarah helped Father Murray to her two seat hatchback. She threw the car in reverse and sped down the driveway. Once out on the road, her pace didn't slow down at all. Even when she passed Sheriff Thompson's patrol car. Her foot didn't even twitch to come off the gas. He never went after her anyway, so what was the point? She hung a left, without slowing down an iota, and flew through the opening in the trees, down the dirt covered drive, up and over the rise to her dad's family farm. They slid to a stop in front. She got out and went around to the back, opening the hatch.

"Need any help?", Father Murray asked, halfway to the house.

"Nah," she said. The hatch sprang open, and she reached in and grabbed the Tupperware bowl of homemade chicken noodle soup that Mrs. Leonard had made for them earlier. She said it was an old family recipe, perfect for getting rid of the creepy crud. "Go on inside and to the kitchen. I will have this warmed up quickly."

She was carrying the bowl inside, marching toward the kitchen, when she heard the shuffling of papers off to her side. "Dad, what are you doing?"

Positioned behind two stacks of papers at the dining room table was her father, dripping with sweat, but wearing a sweater and a jacket. Dark circles had made a home under his eyes, and several coughs interfered with his attempt to respond. He took a sip from his cup of hot tea and lemon, to clear his throat, before he could finally explain, "I have papers to grade. I feel fine."

"You look like shit."

"Sarah, language please," Edward said, trying to sound parental in between coughs and sneezes.

"Oh, she has been a real sailor tonight. Don't think I didn't notice you took the lord's name in vain back at the farm. Oh, I noticed," said Father Murray, from the kitchen.

Sarah stuck her tongue out at the kitchen door, and Edward smirked.

"Come on, Dad. Mrs. Leonard sent this. She said it would have you two right as rain, whatever that means."

Edward got up from the table and followed Sarah into the kitchen. She put the bowl down on the counter and pulled out a large pot that she placed on the largest burner on the stove. She turned the burner on high and poured the contents of the bowl into the pot.

Edward walked past the stove and looked inside the pot on his way to the table. "What's in it?"

"Chicken, chicken broth, vegetables, noodles, and something green. Maybe that is the special ingredient she talked about."

"Sounds good, I wonder what that ingredient is," said her father. He took another sip of his tea.

"Probably pot," remarked Sarah, which caused her father to choke on his tea. She realized, he was not ready for that response.

Father Murray added. "Eh, that wouldn't surprise me. She always has been a little too happy."

The three of them had a good chuckle at that. Sarah watched the pot and once it started to steam, she spooned out two bowlfuls of the soup and delivered them to the table. "Okay, you two eat up. And no more chasing things when it is pouring rain and thirty degrees out. Do that a few more times and you guys will be ghosts, yourselves." She stood over the two men for a few seconds with her arms crossed. Her scolding look produced the same response from both men, "Yes ma'am."

"Okay, good. I am going to go talk to Jacob about ordering a pizza or something. There probably is pot in that stuff."

2

"Jesus," Sarah muttered, the collar of a pink sweater pinned under her chin, while her hands worked at a furious pace to fold the sleeves against the back. Once in position, she let go with her chin and allowed the top to flip naturally across where she held, into the perfect fold before placing it back on a display table. That was one down, and a dozen or more to go. It was the same every afternoon. School let out and droves of junior and senior girls stormed through to shop with their eyes.

This wasn't the local mall or soda shop, something that was still popular in small town America. At least it was in Miller's Crossing. Ralph's had been open since... well, before the birth of anyone still alive. They passed it down from generation to generation. The inside had seen everything from the radio reports of the battle on the beaches of Normandy, to the internal strife of the civil rights movement, not that Ralph's ever had separate entrances or places for people to sit based on the color of their skin. Fred Ralph didn't believe in that stuff, and when anyone made a comment he always said, "The only colors I care about is the green of a dollar, and the whites of someone's teeth when they smile and laugh."

No, this wasn't Ralph's. This was the place next door to it, one of the three clothiers in the Crossing. All three, like Ralph's, were family-run stores that have spanned generations. Myrtle's dress shop had a problem none of the others had. God didn't bless Myrtle Sanders and her husband, Larry, with children. Though they tried. Lord knows, they tried, and faced heartbreak on two occasions. When people would tell them how sorry they felt for her, she would tell each of them, "God granted me a large family. Every child here is her child." In a way, she was right. If you needed jeans and work clothes, you could go to The Miller's Crossing Haberdashery. The sign outside was as gaudy as it sounded. Inside, only the back corner, with suits, hats, and finer clothes, qualified as haberdashery-ish. The rest of it was just run-of-the-mill jeans and work clothes. A-Stitch-in-Time was its female equivalent. Before the large conglomerate stores had opened down the road in Waynesboro or Valley Ridge, that was the one and only destination for back-to-school shopping for every girl from kindergarten to high school seniors. If you needed something nicer, church clothes, a Christening dress, something to wear to Aunt Mabel's funeral, or for homecoming or prom, it was Myrtle's. She had seen it all, for every child in town, from their baptisms through to the measuring and ordering of their wedding gown, only for the cycle to repeat with the next generation.

When Myrtle became ill, Sarah stepped up from her part-time job and ran the store. This was a temporary situation, or was supposed to be. During the winter of the third year after Sarah's graduation, she took a turn for the worst. By spring, she was gone, and Sarah continued to run the store. Larry Sanders's stopped by the Meyer's farmhouse on a Friday afternoon to talk to Edward. Something that wasn't too odd, as he came over often to talk to Edward about his father and the "good ole days". Edward enjoyed those lengthy chats while sitting out on the porch. They felt comfortable and like home, and brought back memories from his childhood. This visit was different. The smile on his face wasn't the normal cheerful expression that brightened his cheeks and brought light into his eyes. It wasn't a grim expression either, like the one he had seen when Myrtle passed.

He said he had something to talk to him about and, like their conversations before, they sat on the porch and talked. This time without sweet tea, or a batch of Larry's home brew. Larry had an idea, and he wanted Edward's honest opinion. He was old and didn't have the energy his wife had had. In seeing how Sarah was running the store, he proposed making an arrangement to sell her the store. As payment, he would withhold 5% of her pay for the next ten years. Edward did the math, and it seemed fair.

The two of them drove together to the store to discuss it with Sarah, who jumped at it before they finished laying out the conditions of the deal. First, she couldn't change the name, and second, she couldn't change what it was. It still needed to be everything it was for the community that it had been. When Larry had slowed Sarah down enough to talk through the conditions, she didn't hesitate.

In the five years since, both conditions had been honored. Myrtle's name was still up on the front outside, now freshened up with a fresh coat of bright red paint, an honor to the bright red lip stick she had always worn. The surrounding building was white shiplap siding, with a green and white canvas awning over the front window and door. At first, Edward had concerns if she could satisfy the second condition. Not that he discounted his daughter's ability to continue to serve everyone how Myrtle had, but this was more than a shop. This was a place people stopped to talk. A place people went to walk around, just to be seen, and to find out what was going on in town. Edward had never considered his family as celebrities in the Crossing. For the longest time he felt it was the opposite. He believed they were notorious for his and Sarah's part in what people now referred to as the "Reaping". It took most of the eight years since for him to realize that no one viewed him as that, instead the town viewed him as the savior that stopped it. They cast Sarah in a similar light, after she returned from her training at the Vatican, with most stopping to thank her for handling a visitor they had had on their property. This meant the shop was never at a loss of people stopping in to shop, browse, or just talk.

With homecoming two weeks away, throngs of teenage girls invaded the shop daily, all coming in to spy the perfect dress, which they would now spend a few days trying to sell their parents on. While in, they indubitably treated the shop as their personal room and picked up various articles of clothing to check the size, the fit, or just to hold up against them to see if it made their eyes pop in one of the two banks of mirrors in the dressing room. This lasted for an hour or two right after school, with most rushing home in time for dinner or to beat the fall of darkness, which arrived early during the autumn. Sarah never complained about the aftermath. Instead, she maintained a cheery appearance as she re-shelved clothes and prepared for the next day. She remembered when she was their age, which wasn't that long ago, and left clothes around for Myrtle to have to put away. It was all part of the repeating pattern of life. Much like the turning of the leaves before fall, then the snow and frost of winter, followed by the blooming of the flowers of spring, and then the long summer nights, which slowly cool again, and the leaves turn once more`.

"Is the storm clear?"

Sarah looked up from the stack of yellow sweaters and smiled in greeting as the third ding from the bell attached to the door echoed around the store. This bell was the same bell that had announced the arrival of every friend, everyone was a friend, and customer since the store first opened. It also reminded Sarah of the past. "Temporary reprieve. Still have two more weeks until homecoming."

The first friend Sarah made after what she thought was a move to a social desert, Charlotte Stance, formerly Reynolds, asked, "Were we ever this bad?"

Sarah cocked her head and retorted, "Myrtle told me once that this was revenge for all the times we did the same." She put the sweaters down long enough to hug her friend and then placed a gentle kiss on the smiling and cooing baby girl on her hip. "And, one day, it will be your turn to run through the store." Sarah gave her friend an evil look, "And your mommy will be nice enough to come help me refold everything."

"And, I will tell auntie Sarah, she has a better chance of getting me to hunt ghosts with her," Charlotte said, with an equally evil look on her face. "How was last night?"

"Wet. Cold. But easy. Neither gave me any trouble."

"I ran into Mrs. Martsen in the salon today, to hear her talk about it, you would think they were from the devil himself, here to suck her soul out through a straw."

"Just small town gossip. She's a local, but still goes on and on, and... Wait! We were supposed to go together on Saturday." Sarah dropped the long flower printed skirt she was refolding. It landed like a parachute covering the table of matching skirts.

"Oh, I can still go with you. Dan's mom was already watching her while I ran some errands in town. I saw an empty chair when I passed by. I had to do something with these ends. I still need to do something about this color."

That color was something Sarah had always been jealous of, the perfect shade of auburn. Not red, not orange, like the leaves of autumn, but an auburn that contained a touch of brown to soften the red.

"Seriously, I am still going with you Saturday. 3:00 PM, right?"

"Yep," Sarah said, her attention was back on the floral print skirt. This was the last table to straighten before closing.

"Good, I can bask in the glow of your fame. Gives me a feeling of what it is like to be around a celebrity A-lister. A break from mommy world."

Sarah sighed. She seriously doubted any celebrity A-listers went through what she did when she was out around town. Ruthie Day, a woman who did not give the appearance of having the skill to help others look good owned the salon, Perm and Clips,. Her hair was still a fifties style beehive that had some serious altitude. Layers of eyeshadow stood guard over her face against the elements of the world, a battle the elements didn't stand a chance of winning. Just like any salon in any small town in America, Perm and Clips was one of the very centers of town gossip.

Ironically, Ruthie's family had an extensive history of being in the gossip business. When the phone lines were strung through town in 1904, her great grandmother, Ruth, not Ruthie, was the first phone operator. That put her in the cat-bird seat for every morsel of town news, with the latest advancement in technology to distribute that news.

On a normal day, two or three of the five cushioned rotating chairs would be filled by someone with some cream in their hair, foil wrapped, being assaulted by a blow dryer and brush, or looking nervous while being orbited by a woman with scissors clipping away as fast as she smacked on her gum. Ruthie, who hadn't touched a strand of hair since before Sarah had arrived in town, would be holding court for those in the waiting room, who most of the time weren't waiting for a seat and were just there for the show. Delores, Crystal, and Pam were there every day to take care of the customers. Lauren and Lisa were part-timers that were only there a few days during the week, both would be there on Saturday, but probably not on the clock.

When Sarah had an appointment, the waiting room was standing room only, with overflow into any unused rotating chair. All five hairdressers would be there, even though only two were working. Instead of being mobbed by paparazzi photographers trying to catch her with hair dye in her hair, or other embarrassing predicaments, they peppered her for stories and questions. Everyone and anyone wanted to hear a harrowing tale of chasing some devilish horned creature through a swamp, or a battle for someone's soul against dark forces. Her first few visits, including her first when Sharon took her thinking it might be less awkward than her father taking her, she resisted talking much about it. In truth, she wasn't involved in things much back then. Her father and Father Murray handled most of it, and neither talked much about what happened. When she returned back from the Vatican, she became more involved and realized most situations were not that interesting. To appease the adoring fans, she embellished slightly. Even pulling from popular culture movies and books, neither of which anyone in attendance would recognize.

That was always curious to her. This was the one place in all of America, that she knew of, where people not only believed in ghosts, but knew for a fact there were aspects of the spiritual world in ours. A place where it was a part of everyday life, but there was no great curiosity in it. No one spending any significant time reading or studying about that world. Instead, they avoided it. There was the natural love for horror movies most high schoolers shared, but as people became older that seemed to wane. Was it because it was too close to reality for them? That was a possibility she gave a lot of credence to.

With every rule, there is an exception. In Miller's Crossing that exception was eighty-three-year-old Edith Wickerson. A source of stories herself. Many that Sarah found fascinating, as they gave a window into her own grandparents' lives. She was more than interested in the world of the spiritual. It was not the "whys" and "whats" that fascinated her. It was the "who". During every story Sarah would tell, Edith asked for a description of the spectral visitor. She wanted to know if it was someone she knew.

3

Wind whipped the first signs of autumn down State Road 32, or what the residents called Main Street. Red and orange leaves rode the wind like a surfer on a majestic blue wave. They fell to the ground as the brisk breeze passed them by, only to be picked up by the next draft. A cold briskly steely feeling blew in with the winds; the first sign that winter was on their doorsteps, and this was its official knock to let you know it was coming in. Sweaters, sweatshirts, hoodies, and jackets, replaced short sleeves for function, not just a fashion statement.

Sarah opted for both as she walked out of Myrtle's and down the three blocks to the Perm and Clips. No less than a dozen people greeted her by name during her walk. All were people she either went to school with, saw at the shop, or met around town. In a town this small, there was no such thing as not knowing someone. Even in the rare instance you didn't, the learned response still kicked in the same as if it were your best friend. Each time she had to loosen up her arms to let a hand free to wave, but as soon as the wave was done, she folded her arms up as tight to her body as possible to keep the chill from penetrating to her core.

Charlotte was doing the same as she walked up from the other direction. She hunched down and turned her head slightly, to let the cloth of her hoodie take the brunt of the wind. "Global warming my ass," she said as she reached for the door handle to open it. She held it open just a moment, to allow Sarah, who was now jogging stiff-legged the last several feet. Sarah went in first, and Charlotte followed. "When I get home, my daughter will get ice cream out of these things."

Sarah rolled her eyes at the nursing humor, one of Charlotte's favorite subjects to make jokes of. She doesn't see the humor, but everyone tells her to just wait, she will.

"Close tha door, you're letting the cold in!", cried Ruthie. The cold air that snuck in didn't keep her from rushing both of them and giving them a hug before they were barely inside the door. As she released Sarah, the fragrance of the rose-scented perfume she bathed in hung in the air and mixed with the putrid chemical smells of dyes, perms, shampoos, and coffee. Coffee was a must for anyone that walked in the door. Not that it was a must for the person, it was a must for Ruthie. Before a person's butt hit their chair, Ruthie had a cup of coffee in a proper cup, on a proper saucer, ready for them. No Styrofoam here. Sharon told Sarah on her first visit to the salon that no one had ever turned her down. Just take it and say, "Thank you." If you drink it, great. If you don't, great too. Sarah always wondered what would happen if someone turned it down.

Ruthie turned around and bent over the counter where the cash register sat. Her artificially gold-colored blond hair seemed exceedingly tall and brushed the shelf above the counter as she bent down. It disturbed none of the hair products displayed on the shelf. She turned around with a smile plastered on her face and a cup of coffee balanced on a saucer in each hand. Charlotte was the first presented with coffee, which she eagerly accepted, and took a sip of the warm liquid. With a hand free now, she handed the other cup to Sarah, while she guided her to an open chair. "Come right this way. We are all set up for you."

They walked past the counter and register, to the first workstation. Crystal was still blow-drying high school senior, Megan Flink's, hair. Ruthie stopped short and gave both a look of disapproval while she tapped her foot. "Ummmm," she said slightly, below a yell, but loud enough to be heard above the hum of the blow dryer. Crystal turned, saw the expression on Ruthie's face, and turned off the dryer. Megan looked back now and saw the two people standing there, waiting on the chair. With no direction from Crystal, she sprang up from the chair and said, "Hi, Miss Miller," as she moved to the next chair over. No matter how many times this had happened, it still embarrassed Sarah.

While all this was going on, Pam stepped forward and took Charlotte back to the fourth chair, the same chair she sat in for her trim a few days before. The color job was saved for today. It took a while to set, and experience had taught her that salon appointments with Sarah were never quick.

"What we doing today, darling?", asked Delores. The mid-forty-year-old petite woman stood behind her and ran her fingers through her hair. Her fingers were stiff with arthritis and years of work, but the pain didn't slow her down. Once the scissors were on, she was a performer which was why Sarah liked her. Of everyone in the salon, she was the only one who had the appearance that she knew what she was doing. She was also the only one without a fancy certificate from a fancy sounding salon school. All she had posted at her station, which was really the one next to where Sarah sat, was her license from the state of Virginia. She acquired her skills through home-schooling. Her grandmother did hair, her mother did hair, her aunt did hair, and now it was her turn. Handed down from generation to generation. All worked for Ruthie from time to time. When not working for Ruthie, they worked out of their kitchens, trading their services for something else of value.

"Take about an inch off, and can you give me something else?", asked Sarah.

"Something else?"

"Yeah, a little wave, texture or something. I don't want tight curls."

Delores studied her straight black hair and looked up at Sarah in the mirror. "Want something for just a few days, or something that will last a few months?"

"Just a few days," said Sarah.

Delores leaned forward and, with the tenderness of a grandmother, whispered, "What is the occasion?"

There are certain places sensitive conversations should never be had. At church, during a quiet prayer. A quiet movie theatre. A quiet classroom. A quiet anywhere would top that list. A beauty salon is anything but quiet. Ringing phones, a television on with a random entertainment talk show grinding, blow dryers and clippers running, and many conversations all happening at the same time. It is a miracle of modern science how, in all that, a whisper could be heard. Not just heard, completely understood, as if she whispered into the ear of every person sitting there. That miracle of modern science had just happened again, and everyone leaned forward in their seat to hear the answer.

"No occasion," Sarah said. Her head turned toward the gathered gallery to her right, to send the message loud and clear. That was a mistake. In her attempt to cover up the truth, she had forgotten a key dynamic in how women communicate with each other. The more you try to make someone believe something was not a big deal, the bigger of a deal it really was. Her attempt to hide it prompted several conversations focused on speculation of what the "it" was.

"She has a date," spouted Charlotte.

The ability to dispatch ghosts, spectral visitors, and demons with a single look was not something they taught her in her training. The look on her face when she turned toward Charlotte may have qualified her to teach her own master class on the topic. The left edge of her upper lip was furled, and twitched, as did her eyebrow, but not at the same time. Keeping her personal life, what little there was of it, a secret in a small town was a struggle as it was. Add the level and mysticism and celebrity that surrounded her family, she might as well post everything on a billboard. Who needs social media posts?

"We will ask about the boy soon. Even though I feel I know who he is," Ruthie said with a cackle as she sat down. The scene of her laughing among her groupies looked like something right out of Steel Magnolias, a movie Sarah had watched several times with her mom. She wasn't sure who was Old Weezer in the group, and not sure it mattered. "So, I hear you had to take care of two vile creatures all on your own the other night."

"It's not the first time I have taken care of my dad and Father Murray."

The court erupted in laughter, causing a small spray of coffee to explode from Ruthie's mouth. That shot should make them forget about the secret Charlotte let slip. In case it didn't, the yarn she was about to spin, about something very uneventful, would.

"Was one of them wearing a grey seersucker? Ronald passed away on Tuesday, and was wearing that in the casket," asked Edith.

4

The chilled breeze of the day gave way to the frozen gusts of night. It howled as it blew across the open fields around the Meyer's family farm. Sarah pulled her coat tight around her as she walked from her car to the front door, pausing for a moment at the door to look around behind her before she walked in. That pause was something of a family tradition, to do a final check before going in for the night. She saw nothing roaming around, didn't feel it either. She also didn't see her father's car in the driveway. At this late of an hour, it only meant one thing. He and Father Murray were out taking care of something.

When she walked in, the house was dark and quiet. The screams of the wind outside gave it an eerie feeling. A loose shutter on one of the dining-room window creaked and banged, adding to the haunted house feeling. Add in the feeling that something was there with her, watching, and she was convinced that with a little work, they could turn the house into a year-round attraction for those who enjoy that kind of thing. That was an idea she had needled her father about since the days he first told her about the book and the cross. That, and trading in the family car for Ecto-1 from Ghostbusters. Jacob had never understood that joke until she found the movie on an on-demand service and then he was all for it. He also wanted the proton-pack.

The floorboards groaned as she made her way through the house and up the stairs. That was something new, that hadn't happened before, at least not for her. Luckily neither her brother nor father were around to hear it, saving her from the snickers and jokes that would undoubtedly follow.

When her head was even with the second floor landing, she could see ribbons of light coming out around Jacob's bedroom door. She knocked to let him know she was home, but there was no response. She knocked again, and still nothing. The time on her phone said it was late, but not that late, only 11:04. There was no way this kid was already asleep. It was a Saturday night, no seventeen-year-old was in bed before midnight. She cracked the door and found her explanation. Her younger, but much taller, brother was sitting in his padded gaming chair with his feet propped up on his bed. Still wearing his baseball pants from his fall league practice, and a single t-shirt, he was immersed in a battle in the digital space taking place on the screen in front of him, and in the sound transmitted via a headset straight into his ears. She had a few options of how to let him know she was home, but very few of them wouldn't result in him jumping out of his skin. A tap on the shoulder would cause him to spin around and scream. She could blow on the back of his neck until he turned around. The last time she did that, he jumped from the chair to the bed in a single move. Feeling a little evil twinge that siblings often do when it comes to causing a mild level of discomfort to one another, she had an idea and slipped out of her jacket and sent it flying in the air. It descended between Jacob and his screen. The only reaction was his head tilting to the side to keep his eyes locked on the monitor. Then one hand let go of the controller and he handed the jacket back over his head to her.

"Hey sis," he said, too loud for just the two of them.

"Dad out with Father Murray?", she asked.

"Dad is out with Father Murray," Jacob screamed over the sounds in his headset.

Disappointed, she dragged her jacket behind her to her room.

She took a quick shower to chase away the remaining chill of the night, and hopefully the other feeling with it. When she emerged from the bathroom, there were lights on downstairs, and sounds coming from the kitchen. Her father was home again, and she thought she heard the voice of Father Murray.

"Hey, Dad. Hello, Father," she said as she walked into the kitchen. "How was everything tonight?"

"Easy," Edward said as he finished fixing him and Father Murray some coffee. Seeing the two of them sitting at the table in the nook, drinking coffee, was as common as seeing a flower in the spring. Also common was watching the flask appear from inside Father Murray's overcoat, or black coat pocket, and then deposit a little into each cup. Sarah had a taste of that a few times. Why someone would add the taste of paint thinner to perfectly good coffee was a mystery to her.

"Are you sure?", she asked. There was an odor to the two of them, and it had nothing to do with their hygiene, or where they may have been. This was something only she had experienced. No one, not her father, not Father Murray, not anyone at the Vatican, or any other sensitive or keeper. She was told it was probably a way synesthesia occurred in her. Synesthesia was a rare condition where senses fire when a person sees a color, number, or hear a certain sound. It would be like seeing the color blue when you see the number two, or smelling strawberries when you see the color yellow. Neither are truly related, but somehow the synapses fire in a way to cross the senses, and it is consistent. If you see blue when you see the number two, you will always see blue. Sarah had that for certain types of spiritual presences, even the after presence that was sometimes still attached to the living that encountered them. She knew, based on the hint of lemony freshness, not coming from any kitchen cleaners, that the spirit they had dealt with wasn't just a lost soul. Those were blueberries. This was one that put up a little fight, probably charged one of them and contacted their clothing, which is where the after presence she could smell was.

"Pretty much," Edward said. He and Father Murray shared a glance. It was one they shared commonly in a similar setting. Sarah knew she was about to be put through a challenge. Both men looked back at her, with curiosity in their eyes. Edward leaned back in the chair and said, "Okay, how about you tell us how it went?"

"Okay," she said and leaned back against the center island. A single finger poised under her chin as she thought. Her eyes looked them up and down to take in the details. Her father had a love of mystery novels, a few she had picked up and read through, but much later in life than he would have liked. When she was nine, he brought home five Nancy Drew mystery books. Just a look at the covers had her laughing and walking away. In hindsight, they did seem a little immature compared to the Lifetime movies on the television. At this moment, she would humor her father and do her best impersonation of Nancy Drew, or was it Scooby Doo, when they unmasked the culprit at the end?

Her mind built a scene to go along with what she sensed. They were outdoors in a field of freshly cut grass. It was dark, not a leap for her mind, since she knew they were out there tonight. It was a single entity. A middle aged man, who had been wandering around for a long time. It was stubborn, and difficult to disperse. She saw her father making several attempts, each of which angered it. It reached a point where it charged at them. Her father got out of the way, but Father Murray didn't. Also not a leap for her mind. She smelled the contact on him.

A quick glance to checked for any visual clues that would confirm her suspicious, she homed in on the details and presented her case. "Well, I can tell by your shoes, you weren't walking around a swamp, or the woods. There are fresh clippings of grass still stuck to them, showing signs of a kept yard. Probably just cut today."

Father Murray nodded and toasted her with his coffee.

"Since both of you went, it tells me you didn't know what you were getting into, or had concerns."

"You never can be too cautious," said Edward.

Sarah dismissed the fatherly advice with a wave of a hand and, "Psh." Her analysis of the situation continued. The whole time she acted like she was putting together the story on the fly. "I can smell something, so it came in contact with..." her finger pointed in their direction and alternated between each of them. It stopped at Father Murray, "You."

"Guilty," and another nod. "You know, I have a theory about you and smells. If you don't mind indulging an old man?"

"By all means. The floor is yours, professor," said Sarah.

Father Murray took a sip from his coffee and then pushed his body up from his seat at the table. A few cracks and pops in his hips highlighted his progress to a standing position. He walked to the counter where Sarah had been standing, and she took his seat at the table. A quick sniff of his coffee cup put a sour look on her face. It had the same turpentine aroma she remembered.

"I have done a good deal of thinking about this ability of yours, and I think the answer is so easy, we have all overlooked it. To be sure, I did some studying and reading. Did you know there are more documented cases of females with psychic abilities than males? It is an overwhelming margin, when you look into it. Those that are more, what they refer to as sensitive, are by and large women. They're the majority. Throughout our folklore, more witches were women. In fact, there are very few legends of warlocks. Now, that is, if you believe in such fascinations as psychics and witches." He paused and then asked, "Be a good dear and bring me my coffee?"

Sarah got up and took him the chemical concoction that used to be coffee, and then returned to her seat at the table. The old priest took a healthy swig and put the cup down on the island behind him, before returning to his lecture, "There are stories all over the place, of mothers that could sense when something happened to their child. Example after example where the fairer gender was more in tune with the world, on every level, than us uncivilized Cro-Magnon aged men, that walk around ignoring the world around us and wage war against one another. Some may say men are one step above the ape on the ladder of evolution, but women are on their own ladder. I am sure you are probably tired of hearing how you were the first female to ever show signs of this ability. There is no one close to being like you. It stands to reason, how you sense the spiritual world would differ from how your father, his ancestors, or anyone else with the gift would, and... like the psychics and others, you may feel things more intensely. We already know you are more capable than anyone Father Lucian has ever seen. Where your father needs to use the cross to focus and amplify his powers, you do not, at least not entirely."

5

"Keep your eye on it," yelled Edward. Jacob had just taken a swing with all the might his nearly six-foot frame could muster, but he failed to make contact. His father could see his eyes were closed from his seat in the bleachers. Something he had struggled with himself when he was younger. The refrain he had just yelled was something he remembered his father yelling at him too. He found it an unnatural sensation to keep your eyes open and focused on the spot of impact between two items moving at high speed. A collision that would send painful reverberations through the ash wood of the bat and into the tensed muscles of his wrists and forearms. The body's natural reaction was to clench the jaw and squeeze the eyes shut, just prior to the crack of the impact, which most of the time didn't arrive. Edward had experienced the overwhelming joy when his body did as he tried to instruct it, and ignored the instinctual reaction, remaining relaxed but powerful through impact. An impact that occurred in slow motion in his eyes, which allowed him to see the ball distort for the briefest of moments before it changed directions and traveled away. The sensation was rare, but memorable.

Jacob, on the other hand, experienced it far more frequently than his father ever had, but at that moment found himself in a slump. He tried hard, not smart, to pull himself out of the bad habits that crept in and added to the frustration. So far, this slump had lasted a little over a week. Coach Tenison, both the fall league and high school team coach, had worked with Jacob in the batting cage, focusing on his fundamentals. Edward felt the itch to add in his own advice, but didn't want to become one of those overbearing parents, so he let the coach do what he does best. Not to mention, he wasn't too sure what he could add that hadn't already been said. Both the coach and Jacob had surpassed his ability, and whatever he might say could just frustrate his son further.

Another swing and a miss sent Jacob sulking back to the dugout. Edward watched each step as he walked. The coach met him just outside the chain-link dugout and pointed up to his own eyes. Jacob nodded at the instructions and then walked in to take his place on the bench. So far, he was 0-for-3 in the game, but made decent contact with a foul ball during the bottom of the third. Even though it was foul, contact was contact. He would pull through this.

They retired the next batter up, ending the inning. The Miller's Crossing Owls held on to a two run lead heading into the bottom of the ninth. The last hint of the orange line of sunset had disappeared below the horizon about a half hour ago, five or ten minutes earlier than the day before, and five or ten minutes later than it would the next day. The days got shorter from here until the end of winter. Banks of lights high atop poles cast a weird, almost too perfect, light across the field from various angles, which didn't allow a single shadow to appear anywhere. A contrast to the long shadows of the twilight just before the sun set. Edward always enjoyed playing under the lights when he was seven, a rare treat normally reserved for the older boys. It made him feel like a major leaguer. In his mind, the simple metal bleachers with wood planks as seats, were towering stands in a stadium that reached up to the heavens. Those sitting in the stands enjoyed the lights too. They were a sign of protection, and kept what lurked in the darkness away.

An unmistakable whack of an ash bat against rawhide sent a ball flying. It took on a florescent appearance in the lights as it traveled, making it easier to see, easier to track down than during the day. Jacob tracked the fly to deep right field. He positioned himself underneath the ball and made the grab to seal the victory for his team. A few ran in with their arms raised, but Jacob jogged in, tossing the ball back and forth between his glove and his hand. The frustration was clear in his body language.

Parents and fans exited the bleachers to stand behind their team's dugout to gather their child and clear out of the park as quickly as possible. Being outside after dark made everyone uncomfortable in Miller's Crossing. The only thing that made them more uncomfortable than the mystery of what the night might bring, was seeing Edward standing in the grandstands fixated on a spot just beyond the centerfield wall. He hadn't moved yet. No attempt to join the rest of the parents behind the dugout, or to gather up Jacob and head home. Instead, he stood there, which caused a few parents to stop and watch him.

Those that watched didn't feel a sense of relief when he moved. They might have if he had joined the rest of the parents. Instead, he walked through them, slowly, his eyes never left that spot. Dozens of eyes watched as he passed the dugout and continued down the right field foul line, pausing next to the tall yellow pole at the outfield wall. His hand now searched the pocket of his tweed jacket for something. That sent all but one heading to their cars. The one left walked a few feet behind Edward. With the roar of dozens of cars starting up and racing off as fast as they could go behind them, Jacob closed the distance between him and his father.

"Dad, is everything ok?"

"Stay back Jacob."

"I will. I feel it too. It's different," Jacob said, his voice strained.

Different was right. There was the normal chill, cold sweat, and pricks of needles up his spine, but there was something else there. Just above the silence of the night, in the void left by the crickets who, on most nights, would be in full chorus by now.

It was a hum, buzz, or a drone. He couldn't make out which to be exact, it was too silent, but there was no mistaking it, it was there. He could hear it, feel it, and even taste it. It was bitter and repulsive, causing waves of nausea. Something about it reminded Edward of the sound he had heard the first time he had witnessed a portal, but different. It pulsated up and down. Not a tremendous difference in volume between the peaks, but enough to hear it. Enough to have a purpose. Enough to seem alive.

Edward took a few steps into the tree line behind center field. The hum was everywhere, and nowhere, all at the same time. A part of the fabric of time itself, deep inside his physical being, vibrating at the molecular level. The vibration disoriented his soul. There was no focus. Thoughts ran in and out, shaking as they passed through. Like being on a giant tilt-a-whirl at the fair, if it spun faster than the speed of light. It was directionless, further blinding Edward, who had honed his perception of spiritual visitors like an extra sense, and could lead himself by it with his eyes closed, but not this time. There was nothing but the hum as he took step after step into the woods, or what he thought was into the woods. As far as he knew, he may have just spun around in a tight circle around the same tree. With each step he took, the less he knew where to go. There were no glowing or flickering spirits in view. The spinning disk he ran into the last time he heard anything that came close to this wasn't there either. He was consumed and blind. He turned around to look for the glow of the ball field, but only found darkness. The trees weren't there either, except when he bumped into them.

A patch of cold damp mist descended into the woods and assaulted Edward. The gelatinous air was hard to breathe, and burned the surface of his skin. Pain sent his eyes clamping down. Where the darkness and the hum had blinded his senses in a fog of confusion, he was now lost and blind in a real fog. He dropped to the ground to get below it, and found a safe haven of a few inches between the bottom of the fog and the cold damp dead leaves that laid upon the soil. The last remaining warmth of day radiated up from the ground, becoming cooler the instant it struck the night air.

As quickly as it began, the hum disappeared from everywhere and into nothingness. It didn't recede back to its source, or travel away. It dissipated into the ether, leaving Edward lying on the ground. The burning was gone, and he could breathe again. He pushed up from the ground, and an uncomfortable feeling pierced his palm. There was something in his hand and it had sharp edges. He brought it close to his eyes, to spy what it was in the darkness. It was not an unfamiliar object, and one that had been in his hand many times. He just doesn't remember retrieving the cross from his pocket.

A quick look around didn't provide any guidance on how to exit the woods. There was no glow from the ball field, or any signs of life. He called out, "Jacob!" He listened. There was no response. He called out again, this time louder, but still nothing. A check of the ground around him for footprints, or any sign of which way he came in from, was met with confusion and disappointment. There was nothing. No footprints. No disturbed leaves. No signs of anything, except directly under his feet. It was as if someone had placed him there from above.

"Jacob!", he yelled again, but still no response. A fourth attempt to scream for his son was in the works. As he took in a great breath of air to power the scream, he remembered a modern convenience, his cell phone. He pulled it out, but it only added to his confusion. It was fully charged on the drive over to the ball field. A charge that should last him a good twelve hours on a good day, with little use, eight hours if he used it heavily. At the game, he had taken a few pictures and videos of Jacob at bat, but that was it. Mostly it had sat in his pocket. There was no way it could be dead now.

Left with one remaining option, he stared up at the sky to identify the stars. His adoptive father had enrolled him in cub scouts as a way for them to bond. The camping trips were enjoyable, but he never really paid any attention to what his den leader tried to teach them. A fact documented by the lack of badges on his navy blue shirt. Faced with a clear sky, he felt some remorse for not learning anything. He knew he couldn't stay there, and made what could be a genius decision, or one he would regret for a long time. Edward picked a direction and started walking. It must have been sheer dumb luck or divine intervention, but after only fifteen minutes, he pushed through the woods out onto Highway 32. How he got there was a mystery his mind couldn't answer. It wasn't a road that was close to the ball diamond.

Two orbs of light illuminated him from behind, and the rumble of an American V8 closed in on him. It slowed and pulled off the road behind him. The gravel and uneven ground popped under its tires.

"Mr. Meyer, is that you?"

Edward turned around and saw Sheriff Marcus Thompson closing the door on his cruiser.

"Hey, Marcus. Yes, it's me."

The young sheriff, with more energy and youth than normally goes with that title, ran up to him. His cuffs and keys clinked and jingled the whole way. "Are you ok?", he asked, eyes wide with concern and confusion.

"Yep, I am fine. Just a little turned around is all."

"I'll say. I was responding to a call from Jacob. It said you went missing in the woods almost an hour ago, but he said that was at the ball field."

"Yea, I thought I saw something behind the outfield and went to check. Got a little lost."

"A little, you are more than ten miles away."

6

"Where?"

"32. Over 10 miles from the field, according to Marcus. There is no way I walked that far," Edward said. Disbelief dripped from every syllable, and his face.

Father Murray considered the possibilities of what had happened to his dear friend. Edward had called him the night before and explained what happened to him. What he had told him was unlike anything Father Murray had ever experienced, or even heard of. He thought about it the rest of that night to make sense, or apply some sense of logic to it. Both of which rarely existed in this part of their life. He needed to reach out, but with the late hour of the night, those he could talk to would be asleep, people he would only disturb for matters of extreme importance, not that he was sure this wasn't.

The next morning he woke up, tired and groggy. His sleep was restless, as dreams of dark shadowy places with a hum dominated his mind and robbed him of a peaceful rest. He hadn't heard the hum himself, so he wasn't sure if what his mind had constructed in his dream state was anywhere close to what Edward had heard. In his experience, dreams were a mechanism for the subconscious to continue working on a problem. The solution, or insight, they may bring are not tempered by the logic of the conscious mind.

A consultation of his standard texts and notes, yielded no similar experiences. On a whim, with the need for more case studies to consult, he fired up his favorite search engine and googled "paranormal hum". The paranormal aspect of his search term was an assumption but considering who he was dealing with, and where they were, it seemed logical.

The results were anything but consistent. There were several articles on the Tao's hum, an unknown sound phenomenon in a town in northern New Mexico. Medical entries for the various causes of a hum in the human ear, the most common of which was tinnitus. Then there was the hum heard around the world on April 12, 2012. People from Sussex to Madrid, Beijing to Moscow, and everywhere in between, reported hearing a hum from the morning until the early afternoon. The explanations ranged from the paranormal, which explained why it came up in his results, to the less terrestrial. To Father Murray, this didn't seem to be related but, just in case, he made a note of it and moved on.

A few pages in, he found all the conspiracy theories of government radio waves aimed at your brain to steal or control your thoughts. If not that, then it was aliens. The first few articles, showing people wearing skull caps made of tin foil, amused him. Like a viral video of someone taking a fast ball to the crotch. You felt embarrassed and bad that this was funny to most of society, but you couldn't stop watching. There was a limit, though, the teeter totter that was Father Murray's mentality tipped over heavier to the side of embarrassment at the state of some members of our supposedly intelligent society. He couldn't go any further for his own sanity, but for the briefest of moments he wondered if the government was using radio waves to plant the alien conspiracy.

He had one source left, and picked up the phone and placed a phone call. The call lasted a good portion of an hour, but still yielded nothing. He wanted to talk to Father Lucian, someone Father Murray had grown to respect a great deal, and regarded as one of the premiere experts in the world of the supernatural. Those at the Vatican saw him in that light as well, and put him in charge of the training of Sarah, and any other sensitives or keepers. To his dismay, Father Lucian was not available, he was on assignment in Puerto Rico and could not be reached, but he did reach Cardinal Rueben, who was filling in at his post for the time being. The cardinal's English wasn't as good as Father Lucian's, and Father Murray's Italian was nonexistent. Through the communication barrier, Father Murray explained what had happened to Edward. He hoped nothing was lost in the translation. There was no immediate explanation from the cardinal. Nor were they any similar situations he could remember. He promised to search through the archives and get back to him.

"Maybe you were in there longer than you thought," Father Murray proposed as an alternative and more logical explanation.

"No way, I was only in there a couple of minutes. Even if I was, I can't cover 10 miles in an hour."

Father Murray looked at his friend, and smiled in agreement. Then he leaned back against the church pew he was sitting in. The crack and pops of the old oak back echoed among the rafters with a volume that made it sound like the entire building were going to fall down. If it weren't for the generosity of several of the local craftsmen, that thought might not have been far from the truth.

"Well," the old priest cackled, "if we were anyplace else, I would say it was all in your mind." A single finger tapped his temple. "But we are here, and it is us, so... a little investigation is in order."

"I am not sure we will find anything," Edward said. "I went back this morning and walked around just outside the centerfield fence. Nothing, just woods."

"Didn't feel anything, anything at all?"

"No."

The discovery that the event was transitory deepened the mystery. There were no other similar events recorded, and now no way to investigate their oddity. At least not until it happened again.

"How is Jacob?"

"Still dropping his elbow," said Edward.

Father Murray pushed up out of the pew and walked toward the rose line. His eyes focused on the cross, and his mind on the event that Edward had described. When he had asked about Jacob, he wasn't asking about his swing. Well, not only asking about his swing. Jacob had showed signs of the same gift his father and sister shared. Edward was trying to foster it and help him accept it, much as he expected his father would have done with him. Father Murray tried not to interfere, but was there to do his job and provide spiritual guidance, as needed. There was only so much either of them could do for him. This was, in some ways, like a father passing down a trade to his son. Not unlike plumbing or carpentry. Father Murray used this analogy to explain to Edward about his family's past. He ran through several trades as examples until he found one he felt was perfect: woodworking.

Someone can take it up as a hobby. They can even receive a little guidance to refine, maybe even the guiding hand of a father can help them learn a new shape, a new technique. It takes time with a true master, as an apprentice, to master the skill. Jacob was just now learning how to see the grain in the wood. Edward was helping him learn how to create a few rudimentary shapes. A smooth pole. A table leg. A spindle for a staircase. It was just a matter of time before it was time for Jacob to take a trip to the Vatican, like his sister had, to be refined by a master, to create some of the finest etchings and carvings the world had ever seen.

"Maybe I should talk to him. I can keep both his faith and swing on an even plane," Father Murray's mind drifted to his ten-year-old self, where the sound of the crack of a bat was as holy as the best prayer is today. Times were simpler for Sarah, Jacob, and even Edward, then. As time moved on, ages increased and life became more complex, just the nature of the world.

7

"Did a strange voice welcome you in?"

"What do you mean?", asked Edward, in between bites of the soup he had brought from home.

"Well... the story you just told me sounds like something from that old show, you know... The Twilight Zone."

"Knock it off, Mark," Edward said before downing another spoonful of soup. His friend had a point. He hadn't thought about it, but his night out in the woods did resemble something he might see in black and white on that show. Most of his life could.

"Strangest thing I have ever heard, and that is saying a lot around here," Mark Grier said out of the side of his mouth, as he chewed on the leftovers he brought. A big brick of lasagna sat steaming in the microwavable container on the table below him.

This wasn't the first time the two men had sat around a lunch table in the teachers' lounge sharing ghost stories. No one else attempted to join them, but it was obvious to both men that everyone in the room was listening. The tables closest to them were full, and quiet. Not a person said a word. You could tell, based on their body language, their ears were wide open to every word spoken.

The sharing was rather one-sided. Mark told Edward some things that had occurred before he arrived back in town, but he ran out of those stories long ago. Now, Mark dug at Edward for any new stories of his adventures out with Father Murray. Edward gave him the general details of the story in about five minutes. The remaining forty-five minutes of their fifty minute lunch period was filled with question after question, to pull out more details. Some were true. Others, Edward made up. That seemed to stop the questions. It also turned into a bit of a challenge to see what he could get past him before he realized he was being pulled along by a great storyteller. The good news for Edward, whatever his imagination could come up with, no matter how outrageous, was all within the realm of possibilities. He had once considered writing a book, using his experiences as the basis for fictional stories. Even sat down and wrote out a chapter. More like half a chapter. He was just getting going when he received a phone call and had to rush off. A firm reminder of his largest impediment to doing any writing: a serious lack of free time.

"You have been here a long time. Ever hear any weird stories about sounds out in those woods?", Edward asked.

Mark thought for a moment while he chewed and then swallowed what was in his mouth. "Nah, not a one. Not even one of those stupid ones kids make up about creepy houses buried deep in the woods. You know we had one about your old place?"

"Oh, I heard. Trust me, I heard."

"You should ask Father Murray, or some of the other old-timers. John Sawyer is one I would talk to. He knows every old tale around here."

"I talked to the father. Nothing. Not in those woods, or anywhere else around here. Even called some of his contacts at the Vatican. Nothing."

Mark chuckled, first silently, and then louder, before partially choking on the food in his mouth. After a few coughs, and looks from the other teachers in the room, he regained his breath and said, "You are the Jacques Cousteau of the paranormal world."

The white plastic spork that Edward used to eat his soup fell from his right hand and plopped into the microwavable cup. Three drops of the brown broth exploded out, splattering on the table. The table slanted away from the men and the three drops raced in that direction. Leaving a snail trail behind them. Edward grabbed his napkin and wiped up the drops before they reached the edge, "What the hell does that mean?"

"A discovery. You are the first to experience this. This is a 'summiting Everest' moment in the ghost-busting world."

8

In the fall, darkness descended on Miller's Crossing with increasing speed. With the darkness, the coolness and the fog followed. Edward could never put his finger on it, but it was something about these nights he felt connected with. Many of them he spent sitting outside on his porch, reading while drinking a beer. How he wished this was one of those nights.

Mixed along in the fog was a cold drizzling rain. The type of rain that soaked you to the bone, if you weren't sitting up on a porch, enjoying the sound. At that moment, sitting on the porch sounded good to Edward. Sitting anywhere sounded good to him. Instead, he was soaked to the bone, through his overcoat and every article of clothing he had on. Water squished between his toes from the inside of his shoes. Leather was supposed to be impenetrable by moisture. Penetration it had accomplished, by the gallons, as he trudged through the yard outside Leroy McGlint's house.

Leroy and his wife, Gladys, looked on from inside, both dry, both warm. Edward was not alone in his discomfort. Father Murray walked beside him with his head ducked inside his jacket to stem the discomfort. His plan didn't work, either. Nothing would. Nothing, except taking care of what they were here to do, getting back into Father Murray's caddie, and hightailing it out of there.

"It's here," Edward said.

"I know, but where?"

That part confused Edward. There wasn't any place to hide here. No sheds, barns, or other structures. The tree line was way off in the distance, something the McGlint clan had taken care of several generations ago, to clear room for row upon row of tobacco plants. Plants that both Father Murray and Edward took care not to step on. The steady drizzle had soaked the planting areas, creating a muddy ooze that now joined the water squishing between his toes.

In between two of the rows of plants, Edward stopped and looked around. His eyes searched for an answer as he said, "We have made several laps around the property and nothing. It is here, but I don't see it." In the years since he had returned to Miller's Crossing, Edward had never given up on a hunt. Once he and Lewis spent two days straight tracking a spirit through the woods. Edward had felt a level of malice from it he hadn't felt since that night so many years ago, at the high school. When they had finally tracked it down, it was not of the demonic nature he expected, just a spirit with an attitude problem. Whether it was worth the two-day trek, the packed sandwiches they ate for each meal, and the few naps they took in sleeping bags on the cold ground, was up for debate.

"Maybe Leroy can remember where he saw it," mumbled Edward, as he trudged through the mud back up toward the house. The light on the back porch came to life as they approached and sixty-four-year-old Leroy, and his Budweiser can that was now re-purposed as a spittoon, appeared in the doorway. His white hair was a mess, showing evidence of hours under a ball cap during the day. The sweat stains in the tee-shirt under his unbuttoned flannel shirt told of the day he had spent in the field, tending to his plants. Several farmhands helped to work his farm, a necessity on the seventy acre farm. That didn't keep Leroy from working it alongside them though. Something he would probably do until his body wouldn't allow him to anymore.

"Cold out here," pointed out Leroy from his spot on the dry stoop, under a roof overhang.

Edward was just about to ask Leroy where he had last seen the nuisance, but held up a hand that stopped all three men in their tracks. Silence hovered in the surrounding fog, with only the music of the rain drops playing in the background. Edward's head turned. He felt something as they walked back to the house, and it was stronger there at the porch.

He backed up and looked at the roofline of the house and walked from one side to the other. There was nothing there except the drain vents and an old antenna, bolted to the side of the red brick chimney. He walked back to the back door, where Father Murray had taken a break in their search to join Leroy on the stoop under the roofline. Both men looked inquisitively at Edward as he continued to search.

Edward asked, "Leroy, do you have a door to your crawl space?"

"Yes sir, right around thar," he said as he spat into his makeshift spittoon. His right hand lifted the can to meet the stream of brown liquid and motioned around to Edward's right.

Around the corner, to the right, Edward found what he was looking for. In the brick foundation, there was an iron door, hinged into an iron frame, mortared into the bricks. He knelt down and twisted the simple handle, which moved a metal bar on the back side out of a catch. It squealed as it turned. As he pulled back, the door scraped against the frame, and the hinges resisted his attempt to open it. He pulled harder and a cloud of rust exploded from the hinges with a pop as the door squealed open. The sound sent a chill up his already tingling spine. With the flashlight he had been using all night to search the property in hand, he poked his head inside the door and then pulled out and sat, leaning against the bricks.

"What is it, Edward?"

"It's there."

"Okay, then, let's get this over with." Father Murray urged him to go on in there with both of his hands.

"With mud... and lots and lots of spiders," Edward said as he stared out into space. A panicked look was painted on his face.

"So, go on."

"I don't like spiders. I REALLY don't like spiders."

"Let me get this right. You can chase ghosts all day long, but you don't like spiders?", asked Father Murray. He crouched down and looked in through the door, into the crawl space. The land on the east side sloped toward the house, sending a flood of water underneath it, creating a bog in the cramped area. No more than fifteen feet in, sat a single spirit, a woman, just sitting there on the ground, like she was enjoying the sun in an open meadow. "Doesn't look that bad."

Edward held the flashlight out for Father Murray. He took it and directed the circle of light. He let out a great sigh and joined Edward, sitting on the ground next to the door.

"Maybe it is just a lot of webs."

Edward looked at him, crossed. Under the house, the two-by-eight floor joists were not visible behind the layer of spider webs that descended each footing to the ground.

"Well, it's in there," said Father Murray. "Explains why we could feel it all around the house."

"Yep," was all Edward could muster in response.

"Someone has to go in there and deal with it."

Edward leaned over and looked through the hole. He didn't need the flashlight. The flickering of the woman illuminated the webs around her. They appeared to dance from their attachments to the house. It could be just the wind. That would be the logical explanation. Edward's mind had a different one though. In his mind, hundreds or thousands of spiders walked along each strand, causing them to bounce, like an army walking across a bridge. His skin could feel their tiny hair-covered feet walking up his arms.

As he returned to his seat on the wet ground against the brick foundation of the McGlint house, he proposed an alternative that took only seconds to rationalize in his head. "You know, she doesn't look like she is hurting anything. We could come back tomorrow, or never."

Edward heard the unamused chuckle from his partner in crime. No other reply was necessary, and he pulled out the cross and book from his pockets, then prepared himself to enter the void. Father Murray offered him the flashlight, which Edward considered taking, but eventually refused. He hoped to find a reprieve in the logic of a small child: what he doesn't see can't hurt him.

Within the first few feet he crawled, that axiom was proven untrue. His hands and knees were caked and covered in squishy mud, and he had run into several webs with his face, no matter how low he tried to get to duck under them. They stuck to his forehead, as if they were covered in glue. He didn't see them, but he knew they were there, just above his eyebrows. Every second they felt like they fell closer to his eyes, even though they hadn't moved. In his mind, dozens of tiny spiders were now walking around in his hair. His scalp crawled in response.

He kept on toward the woman. She paid no mind of him. He held the cross toward her, and she didn't move. She sat there, not motionless. Her head moved back and forth as she studied something in her lap. There was a delicateness to her expression and motion, much like a young girl brushing the hair of a baby doll sitting in her lap.

As sympathetic as he could manage, while covered in mud, with a thousand spiders marching on every synapse of his brain, he said, "I free you to join your loved ones in His eternal garden."

She flickered twice more before she never came back. Edward turned around and rushed out through the webs. This time, he did not try to duck under them, and resembled something more akin to Godzilla walking through a Japanese town. When he emerged through the door, he collapsed on the ground and rolled back and forth in the mud. His hands were a blur as they tried to brush whatever was in his hair, and everything that wasn't, out. When satisfied the webs, and imaginary spiders, were gone, he stood up. A random tingle on his skin, probably just psychosomatic, sent his hands rushing to chase whatever it was away. The webs were all gone, as were the spiders that never were there, but mud covered him from head to toe.

"Leroy?", called Father Murray, from where he sat along the foundation of the house.

Leroy emerged from around the corner of the house, a hand held up to shield him from the rain, his head ducking to the side to avoid the drops that made it past his hand. "Yes, Father," the annoyed man said.

"Got any plastic? Edward isn't getting into my car like that."

***

"What the hell happened to you?", Jacob asked.

"Language, son."

Jacob was lounging on the sectional couch in a pair of grey sweatpants and a Senator's t-shirt. An action film with several loud explosions played on the television. He reached down for the remote and adjusted the volume to avoid another corrective instruction from his father. He had a hand full of chips from a bowl that sat on the floor and was stuffing them into his mouth when Father Murray walked through the door behind him. A smirk was on his face.

There was no such smirk on his father's face. His expression could only be described as miserable. He was wet. Rivers of mud ran down from his hair, across his face. Drops of a thick brown fluid dripped from his coat to the floor.

"I am not cleaning that up," said Sarah. She had just returned home herself, and stood there gawking at the scene now midway between the front door and the door to the kitchen. Like Father Murray, she had a smirk on her face. Her father turned toward her to give her a full view of his expression.

"It was under a house. Your father had to crawl through the mud to get to it," explained their family priest.

"And SPIDERS!", added Edward.

"Oh, yes, we can't forget the spiders," chuckled Father Murray.

Now three of the four in the room were laughing uncontrollably.

"There were thousands of them, and they were big," pleaded Edward.

"Let me get you some towels," Sarah said in between giggles. "You couldn't hose him off before you brought him home."

"Well, I thought about that, but Leroy uses reclaimed sewage water for his crops."

Sarah stopped in her tracks and looked at the brown puddle around her father's feet. The giggling stopped, and a look of repulsion replaced it. "Please tell me..."

"That is mud. Trust me, that is mud. He didn't hose me off," interrupted Edward.

The news did little to change the disgusted look on her face as she squeezed past him and up the stairs. Jacob was still planted on the sofa, but had contorted his body to keep the attraction firmly in his view. Edward was sure this would become one of the many family moments his kids would remember and bring up years later for a good laugh.

Sarah emerged from upstairs carrying several towels in her arms.

Jacob's "How was the date, sis?" question drew her ire in the form of a rolled-up towel fired at his head.

"Oh, there is someone special?", asked Father Murray.

"Just dinner Father."

"Do we know him?", he asked.

"In this town? Would it be possible for you not? It was Kevin Steirers. No point in hiding it."

9

The light of the midday sun shone through the window in the breakfast nook and across the table, casting a large irregularly shaped shadow upon the tile floor. Its normal shadow resembled a flat table, but the one today had square items protruding from the top of it, like a distant mountain range made of a child's building blocks. The objects casting the shadows were not blocks or boxes, they were stacks upon stacks of newspapers. It wasn't time for the great paper drive, like the ones Edward remembered from his elementary school days. For those, his family would store every paper, every piece of junk mail, anything made of paper, for months, to help his class gather the most paper, by weight. Of course, that was all for a little 9-inch trophy.

Edward was not sure if they still did that at the elementary school. He wasn't sure if they still had newspapers. He couldn't remember the last time he had read one, or a current one, that was. Stacked before him were yellowed, and partially rancid smelling, copies of the Miller's Crossing Ledger from thirty years ago or more. All before Edward had left town. Father Murray had collected them and stored them in his garage, as a scrapbook. Each paper had a story about Father Murray, and either Edward's Father or grandfather, dealing with some supernatural occurrence around their small town. Now none of them documented what they were really doing. A fact that Edward found rather humorous and prompted more sighs than laughs from Jacob.

The cover stories ranged from rampaging livestock, to chickens that refused to lay any eggs, or crops that wouldn't grow. Edward's father, or grandfather, were there to provide guidance and expertise as a town elder, to help the stricken families. Father Murray, on the other hand, was there to pray for the dead crops, or spooked cow.

"Oh, look another story about a pig that won't eat," cackled Jacob.

Father Murray leapt up fast for his age and read the story over his shoulder. He reached over and snatched the paper off the stack, to look at the date, July 4th, 1954. A smile slowly crept into his eyes. Eyes that were now drifting years away into the past, as he had remembered the true story of that day. "That, my boy, was the day your great-grandfather, and me took down two while fireworks went off over our heads and everyone watched on. Not particularly challenging, at least not for him, but different. We never had an audience before. Afterward, everyone tried to offer us a piece of pie, or whatever dessert they had brought with them to the city's Independence Day picnic. It took me weeks to work off all that weight."

Jacob looked at him, his expression odd and quizzical.

"I am a man of the people. I couldn't turn them down, now could I? I sampled each."

Jacob asked, "Why aren't there stories about that?"

"Well... there are. If you read, I think they even asked me whose pie was best."

"That is not what I meant."

"Outsiders," said Edward, from the other side of the table, where he was busy reading other stories. Some were ruses like that one Father Murray was discussing with Jacob, but others were actual stories. Real insights into the town's past and his family. Outside of what Father Murray could tell him, reading a story on the sports page about his father's high school career, or quotes from his grandfather about some great issue up for debate among the town elders, were his only sources to learn about his past, and who the legendary men that had preceded him were. It was fortunate that his family played a significant enough role in the town's history to allow those stories to overlap each other, more fictionalized events, making these saved treasures a true window into his past.

Time had started to rob him of the few memories he had had from the first seven years of his life. A sign of the progression of time that Edward couldn't stop, no matter how bad he wanted to. Now, more than ever before, he wanted to remember, for him, and to tell his children. It was important to him for them to know his family. The tragedy of his childhood had taken that chance from them. A chance they needed, in his opinion, more so than most families. His children needed to know their heritage. They needed the lessons of the past. They needed to know who those family members were, that walked this path before them, and what they were like. All of this would help them handle their gift better. It had to, he hadn't had that chance, and had struggled immensely.

"Hey, Jacob, here is one on your grandfather's three touchdown game," said Edward as he tossed a paper on top of the stacks in front of his son. It fanned the odor of mildew and mold out when it landed.

What he had learned so far was, his father was who he remembered: a fiery but fair individual, with a desire to help anyone and everyone. Just like he remembered, his father and mother were involved with every aspect of community life. What was obvious was, this must have been a quality instilled into him by Edward's grandfather. Story after story presented Edward with the image of a man who was bigger than life, and this small town. The way he discussed community matters in the paper resembled a seasoned diplomat, with a lean toward being a national politician.

"*The need to repave the route 281 log road might not be obvious to everyone, on the surface, yet these are the little things we need to do as a community to thrive,*" *said Alderman Carl Meyers.* "*You may never drive on the route, but you do derive benefits from it. The logging companies contribute to the financial wellbeing of our town. Just last year, they hired thirty-two locals. Thirty-two jobs we would not have otherwise. The more we improve the route, the better our chances of attracting other companies into our fertile land, bring more opportunities. Not to mention, the money they spend while here, at the local diners, stores, and gas stations. It supports our local business owners and contributes to our tax coffers. Over the next week I will be working with those in opposition, to address their concerns.*"

Story after story, were the same. His grandfather was quoted on every significant issue, and even just town gatherings. Wherever he was, the reporters, or reporter, would find him, and he always had something great to say. At that moment, but not for the first time since he had returned home, the shoes everyone looked for him to fill felt way too large for his feet.

"Knock. Knock."

Edward looked up from the report he was reading from the annual fall festival, that occurred during the day before Father Murray and his grandfather rushed a spirit from the gazebo in the town square. "Hey, Lewis. Come on in."

The now-retired sheriff stepped in through the backdoor. A minor hitch in his giddy-up caused by a touch of rheumatoid arthritis in his left knee and hip. Something that always bothered him, and got worse in the cold Virginia winters. His red and blue flannel shirt, jeans, and "Rather Be Fishin'" hat advertised his now retired status. Walking in behind him was his younger, more able-bodied, replacement, who had moved up from deputy to Sheriff after the encounter at the portal sent him into an early retirement.

Marcus Thompson was a good sheriff. He was honest, trusted by everyone, and eager. The eagerness was something Lewis worked to temper in him while he was still his deputy, and then after during their many conversations, once he was promoted. He was a local boy, born and bred. His father was a deputy on the force before him. That probably led to some of the romantic allure that line of work held for him. One might think, with a father that was in it, he would have been better prepared. He had the skills, but started out a little too idealistic and less understanding that this was a small town, a tight-knit community. Sometimes you let little things slide. If you see two friends fighting and shoving, maybe it is best to just step in and send them on their own way, instead of slapping cuffs on their wrists and bringing them down to sit in the two jail cells they had at the station. This had happened a few times, mostly involving a few of the older residents that had had a bit too much of the homemade fire-water. Each time it happened, Lewis would unlock the doors and let both men walk out with a stern warning of, "You both should know better... now don't end up back here again." If Lewis had been the one to see them doing whatever Marcus had thought they were doing, he would have issued that same warning on the street and sent them separate ways, or given each of them a ride home to end it right there and then. He eventually learned and loosened up to become a well-seasoned law man, even if his babyface didn't look it. His clean-shaven look missed that lawman mustache that Lewis had so proudly sported throughout his entire career. He continued to sport it today, but the only thing he had been taking into custody lately were carp.

"I smell something old."

"Must I remind you, Lewis, we are about the same age," sniped Father Murray.

Lewis picked up a paper from the top and began flipping through it. Marcus did as well. "Where did you find these old things?"

"I kept them. A chronicle of sorts. Figured Edward might like to read about his family."

A deep belly laugh welled up inside of the former sheriff's rotund frame. It surged up and out and filled the room. The laugh was so large, the action of releasing it forced his arms to move and shake the paper, causing the dried and aged paper to crinkle. "We had to come up with some doozies as cover stories, didn't we?"

"That we did. I figured you and I could fill in the truth behind each of these," said Father Murray.

"I imagine we would have to, but that needs to wait for another time. My young friend is here on official business."

With that, both Father Murray and Edward put down the paper they had in their hands. Jacob kept the one he held in his hand, but looked over the top edge of it at the sheriff. Those words added a tension to the room.

"How can we help?", Edward asked, his attention now focused on the young babyfaced sheriff.

"I need to speak with Sarah, Mr. Meyer," he said. Each hand hooked on a belt buckle on the sides of his waist.

"Sarah, why? Father Murray and I can help..."

"It's not something like that," he interrupted. There was a quick glance at Lewis before he continued, "Is she home?"

"Yes, let me get her." Edward got up and headed out the door to get Sarah. She was up in her room, watching television and finishing up some laundry, before heading in to work in the boutique later that afternoon. When Father Murray had arrived with the papers, they had invited her to come take a look with them. Something Edward had hoped she would have shown more interest in. Her reply was, "No, thank you. I spend too much time dealing with things from the past."

"Sarah," he said, as he knocked on the door.

"Yeah, Dad," she replied through the closed door.

"Can you come down for a bit?"

"I told you. I am not interested in looking through a bunch of old mildewed newspapers."

"It's not that. The sheriff is here. He wants to talk to you."

There was no verbal reply. Just the sound of footsteps approaching the door, followed by the creak the door made as it opened. When she stepped out, she was timid and looked at her father inquisitively. "Why?"

Edward just shrugged and led her downstairs.

10

Edward followed Sarah into the kitchen. Sheriff Thompson was the only person still standing. He was there in his cop pose, his thumbs still hooked into the belt loops on his pants, just as Edward had left him. Plastered on his youthful face was an attempted scowl. This was not a skill he had mastered. Instead of being intimidating, he looked like he had a burrito or chimichanga at lunch that was riding low in his intestines. Lewis Tillingsly, on the other hand, had a scowl that could make the earth quake. Even with his large cookie duster covering most of his mouth. It was the eyes. The narrowing of the eyes and the lean of the eyebrows. Neither of which looked menacing on Marcus.

When Sarah saw the assembled group in the kitchen, she froze in her tracks. There was a concerned look on her face. Edward shared the same look. Even though he considered everyone there a friend, there was a slight feeling of having walked her into an ambush.

"Sarah, take my seat," Lewis said as he leaned his weight forward and pushed himself up.

When she walked toward the now vacant seat at the table, Marcus stepped in behind her, before Edward could pass, closing the proverbial door. Edward moved around and stood off to the side, next to the large marble-covered island. Sarah's lips had a tad of a quiver to them.

"Jacob, why don't you go on into the other room and let us talk to Sarah?", suggested Edward. He could tell Sarah felt uncomfortable. No need adding to it, having her little brother there gawking at her from across the table during whatever this was.

"Sarah, I need to ask you a question," began Marcus. "When was the last time you saw Kevin Steirers?"

"Um... last night. Why?"

"Where was that?"

"At Len's, we had dinner together," she said, and again looked around the room for acceptance of her answer from those assembled.

"When?", the sheriff asked, coldly.

"Well, we met there around 7 and ate. Afterward, we stood outside and talked. We were still talking when Len closed things up just after 9, but left in our own cars not long after. Why? What's up?"

"Are you sure about the time you guys left? Was it closer to 9 or maybe 10?", he asked.

This time Father Murray answered on her behalf, "Had to be closer to 9. She walked in just after we got home, and that was before 9:30." His response brought a look from Sheriff Thompson, and Father Murray clenched his mouth shut and leaned back in his chair.

Edward noticed the look, and Father Murray's response, but didn't let either deter him. "Marcus, what is this all about?"

"Just asking some questions," he said, keeping his look stern, and the lid closed on sharing any additional information.

Lewis's eyes studied his replacement and then threw the lid right off. "She's not in any trouble or anything, Edward. Kevin was found wandering around Harper's Hill Road early this morning, dazed, confused, and all scratched up. Frank Tyler passed him, loaded him up in his truck, and brought him to me. The kid seemed completely out of it. No clue where he was. No clue who he was. No clue where his car was. No clue how he ended up in the passenger seat of Frank's truck. When he was transported to the hospital, Wendy Nyles said she saw him having dinner with Sarah last night, wearing the same clothes."

"Is he okay?", Sarah asked. The quiver was gone from her lips and voice, replaced by compassion and a great deal of concern.

"Hard to say. He was still pretty out of it when I left him. Did you guys have anything to drink last night?"

"No, Len's doesn't sell any alcohol," said Sarah.

"I hate to ask, but I have to, Miss Meyer... any drugs? Maybe a little pot or something?", interjected Marcus.

Sarah's head whipped side to side as she declared, "No!"

"I had to ask," Marcus said sheepishly, as he looked at the others in the room.

Father Murray placed a comforting hand on Sarah's shoulder and asked, "Lewis, do you think this could be... unnatural?"

"Don't know, Father. The thought crossed my mind."

Marcus nodded in agreement, with a look on his face that screamed, *"I don't know!"*

Edward looked at Father Murray and suggested, "Maybe we should talk to him?"

"I wish you would," Lewis said. There was a little stir in the room, and the sound of rustling next to Edward, as Marcus shifted his weight from side to side, and then his posture, as if to remind the men in the room who was really in control of such matters. Everyone, including Sarah, noticed and focused their attention on him. Among the men old enough to be his father, he still appeared to be a child trying to make sure he had his father's attention. Regardless of his age and actions, he was the sheriff, and Edward knew this was his responsibility. If he wanted them to talk to his victim, then Marcus would have to be the one to ask. It appeared Lewis remembered that, too, "If that is ok with you, Sheriff?"

"No objections. I appreciate any help you gentlemen can provide."

Father Murray slid the chair out and squeezed past Sarah. His large black brimmed hat sat on the island in the center of the kitchen. He picked it up and placed it firmly on his head, saying, "We can take my car."

"Now?", asked Edward, with a tone of mild surprise.

"Of course. Whatever has him might not be there later, plus... if it is something like this, he could be suffering and need our help now." Father Murray headed out of the kitchen, toward the front door. Without a word, Sheriff Thompson and Lewis Tillingsly headed for the back door they had entered a few minutes earlier. This left Sarah and Edward in the kitchen, in silence. It was an awkward one, which confused Edward. Having the local sheriff in his kitchen in times of emergency was not a unique occasion. It happened more than he liked, but it was life. This was the first time one of his children was the target of questioning, though.

"Edward, are you coming?", Father Murray called from beyond the kitchen door.

"Yes, Father," replied Edward. He turned around and headed toward the door.

"I am coming, too," said Sarah. As Sarah rushed by him for the door, Edward considered stopping her. Half of him didn't think this was a good idea, but the other half knew how skilled and perceptive she was. If there was something unnatural going on here, she may be able to help in ways neither he nor Father Murray could.

The ride to County General was quiet, with no sound except the occasional squeak of the old suspension, and the odd cricket-like chirp the speedometer made as it approached 55 miles per hour, a speed well over the posted speed limit. They pulled into the parking lot of the hospital just as Lewis and Sheriff Thompson were getting out of their patrol car. They all walked in together and down the front hall, toward the Emergency Room where Kevin was still being treated.

"You guys wait here for a moment," asked the sheriff who went ahead to the nurse's desk. After a few minutes of discussion with her, he returned to the group. "Okay, he hasn't improved and is very confused. They asked that we be gentle. Father. Edward. Come with me."

Sarah moved forward with them, but Lewis brushed her arm around the elbow to catch her attention. He shook his head "No" and then looked over at a row of chairs lined up against the wall as a makeshift waiting area in the small hospital's emergency department.

The sheriff led Father Murray and Edward through a break in a light blue curtain. Behind the curtain lay Kevin Steirers, on a hospital bed, now wearing a green gown, and looking straight up at the drop ceiling. Neither his eyes, head, nor body, made any motion to acknowledge their presence. The three men gathered around the hospital bed and trained their eyes on him, much like a doctor would do to diagnose him.

"Kevin, these men are here to talk to you," said the sheriff. Kevin didn't even twitch.

"How are you feeling, Kevin?", Father Henry asked. Still nothing.

Edward didn't spend long looking at the blank expression on his face before his attention roamed to the dozens of large swatches of bandages all over the exposed area of his body. There was no evidence of blood seeping through from underneath. On his right arm, someone had removed the bandages from one of the rows of three scratches. Each was long, and several layers of skin deep. Edward didn't have a logical explanation for what had made them, but he knew whatever it was wasn't human. It could have been an animal, he thought. Lots of bobcats, badgers, and even bears in the area that could have done that to him. There was one problem with that theory. If that type of animal injured you in that way, the chances that you would get away and not be chased and eventually killed by them was slim-to-none. The injuries, themselves, were grave, no matter the source. The skin around each scratch was cut clean, like a razor blade slashed it. It showed an almost surgical precision. The gouge in between each edge was something different, something more primal and violent in appearance. It had ripped the tissue down to the muscle. Even cleaned up, it gave every appearance of being infected, with small pockets of pus leaking into the middle of the gouges, creating a river of ooze.

A nurse rushed in and squeezed in between Edward and Father Murray. In her right hand was another roll of bandages that she quickly wrapped around the exposed wounds on Kevin's right arm. She finished the wrap and tightened it. With expert precision and speed, she applied strips of paper tape along the edges of the wrapping. Both hands ran along the tape to ensure proper adhesion to both the bandage and the skin. Edward watched as she worked, and expected to see the evidence of blood and pus soaking into the bandage she applied, but it didn't. It stayed as white and pure as it had before she placed it over the wound. She left the room, but not before making eye contact with all three men. Her eyebrows drawn close together.

"Are they running blood tests?", asked Father Murray.

"Thinking drugs?", asked Sheriff Thompson.

Father Murray just nodded agreeably.

"Yep."

"Kevin. It's Father Murray, can you hear me?"

Just like before, Kevin laid there. His face flaccid, only held up by the bones underneath. Eyes looked attentively out, but not at any of them, or anything in the room. They were focused, and didn't move. Outside of the slight rising and falling of his chest, there was no movement, even when Father Murray placed his hand on his forehead.

Edward watched as the priest's thumb drew a tentative cross on the young man's forehead. He hoped for a reaction. That would make it easy. They knew how to deal with demonic presences. There was nothing, not even a flinch. This was not spiritual, or at least not some kind of spiritual control. He may have still encountered something out on the road, or in the woods, that night that had put him into shock. The scratches fit into that scenario.

"I am not sure, Sheriff. This may be completely medical," Father Henry reported, somewhat disappointedly.

"Did you see the scratches?", asked Edward.

"No. Why?"

"You need to. Can we ask a nurse to show us?", Edward asked Sheriff Thompson.

The young sheriff stood there and considered the request, before walking out of the room, his eyes still locked on the victim. It didn't take long before he returned, followed by the same nurse. Edward could tell the request didn't amuse her, but she complied all the same. She peeled back a bandage on his left arm. Edward surmised she didn't want to redo the one she had just replaced on his right. When the deep cuts and gouges came into view, Father Murray gasped, "Dear God." He moved forward to get a closer look.

Edward noticed the lack of seepage on that bandage, as well, and was astonished after seeing the amount of fluid that was underneath. This put a new target in his head for investigation, and he searched the room, finding a small bag on the floor containing the jeans and black cotton button-up shirt he had to assume Kevin was wearing when he was brought in. He slipped the clothes out of the bag to investigate, keeping his back turned to the sheriff, to hide what he was doing. There was no desire to be caught possibly tampering with evidence. The sweet Jasmine smell of his daughter's favorite perfume wafted out. That wasn't surprising to him. What was, was what was missing. His shirt was dry. With all the cuts and scratches, it should have been soaked in blood, but it wasn't. There wasn't even a single dried discolored stain around the slashes in the material. Edward quickly shoved both back in the bag and returned it to the floor.

Behind him, the nurse was securing the tape and bandage back on this skin, when Kevin's head shot toward the door. It was not a smooth turn, more of a jerk, a single move, from facing forward to facing the door, in under a second. His eyes didn't blink, but had another target to fixate on. Edward followed his gaze and saw Sarah's head poking through the door. Kevin's body quivered ever so subtly.

11

Sheriff Thompson walked the others outside to the parking lot. They hadn't learned a lot, or anything from visiting Kevin. In Edward's opinion it had equal chances of being an animal or something from the natural world, as it did of being something from another world. The scratches still stuck out to him, but Lewis told the story of someone he had once seen with similar deep cuts after a run-in with a black bear, a native to these parts. It was a possibility Edward had to consider.

"Odd, very odd," remarked Lewis, as they approached their cars to leave.

"Yep, even for here," said Marcus, who then added, "this might take over-the-top spot from the animals in my list of strangest things this week."

"What animals?", asked Father Murray.

"Oh, it's nothing, Father. A couple of hunters saw the desecrated bodies of a few squirrels hung in the trees. Their heads posted on sticks. Probably just kids, but worrisome. You know most of the great serial killers started off with something similar."

The sheriff was correct on that point. Edward had seen a few documentaries on television about Jeffrey Dahmer that talked about his bucket of "fiddle-sticks". Seems his childhood involved helping his father, a professional chemist, bleach the tissue off the bones of the rodents they caught under their house. They kept the bones in a bucket that was affectionately termed his own "rattle". While, in hindsight, his family tried to cast that off as scientific curiosity, they couldn't explain the impaled dogs' heads, or other acts that occurred in his later years.

Edward knew you could never predict who would turn into such a monster. That was always the biggest question on such shows. It was hard for him to consider someone here in Miller's Crossing being that demented. There was another explanation, outside of just doing something stupid and mischievous, which was not completely out of the range of possibilities here. That option, to him, was even a bit darker than becoming the next serial killer. That was the occult.

The locals all knew the history of this place, and what it meant. It had caused a few to become more religious than you might find in most towns. Something Edward felt was relatively natural, all things considered. He, and the others, would be naïve not to consider the chance that someone might become just as fascinated in the other side. It was a topic he had recently spent some time researching. Not out of some desire to switch sides, but to gain an understanding of the other side. It was Sun Tzu that said, "Know thy enemy."

"Where did they find them?", Edward asked, breaking his silence since pointing out the scratches to Father Murray. The four others looked at him, surprised at his interest. "There is another reason someone may have done that."

The surprised looks on the other four faces was replaced by ones of deep concern, as their eyes dropped from looking at each other, to looking at the cracked rough pavement with faded lines of yellow paint.

"Edward, you can't think it would be that. Not here?", pleaded Father Murray.

His friend's argument took aback Edward. Of all people, he expected Father Henry to have already made that leap himself. "We can't discount anything, Father," he said and then turned his attention to Sheriff Thompson. "Where abouts did they find them?"

"I can take you, if you would like?"

"Okay," Edward agreed.

"I'd best come along too," said Father Murray.

"Me too," said Sarah.

"Oh, no," objected Edward.

"If it is what you think it is, you will need me," she argued.

She had a point, and Edward knew it. She was more capable in these dealings than he was, and the formal training she had received from Father Lucian covered the occults. Edward's knowledge was what he could gleam from the internet and a few books he had downloaded on his tablet. Not wanting to seem like she had won, Edward didn't agree, nor did he provide another objection.

"Well, let's go. Just follow me, Father," said Sheriff Thompson.

Lewis rode with Marcus, and Sarah and Edward took the white-knuckled ride with Father Murray. It wouldn't be too much longer before Edward had to have a conversation with the father about giving up his driving privileges, or maybe going to something a little smaller and more modern. His old Cadillac's suspension swayed back and forth from white line to yellow line. Each of his over corrections sent the car drifting over the line. A few involved a daredevil dive toward several old oak trees that had grown close to the edge of the roadway over the decades. Many were obviously placed by the devil, himself, on the edge of the blind hairpin turn. Scuffs of paint stood as warnings of past battles with motor vehicles where the car had lost.

About six miles outside the center of town, the two cars pulled off to the side of the road. The ground was still sloshy after the torrential rain from a few nights ago, allowing the car tires to sink in slightly. It squished under each footfall as Edward followed the sheriff off into the woods. The rest followed behind them. The underbrush was thick, which made the going rough. It would be a few weeks before the first hard freeze of the year knocked down the lush weeds and bit back some smaller plants.

Edward kept his mind clear, or as clear as he could, so he could sense if anything was out there. So far, he had felt nothing, only heard the pop of a twig or a leaf a few times. Each one he dismissed as a small animal moving about, they were in their environment. That thought sent a shiver down his spine, they had all been stupid. Bow hunting season had opened a few weeks ago, and not a single one of them had thought about putting on something brightly colored to avoid being confused as an animal. He was about to comment on that when Sheriff Thompson stopped and said, "Here it is."

Here it is, was right. Edward expected to see just a few squirrels hanging from a branch, and a head or two pushed down on a stick. The scene he just walked up on sent a shiver all the way up and down his spine, and out through his arms and legs. "Think I am off-base now?", he asked.

Father Murray replied with a hesitant and mortified-sounding, "No. Absolutely not."

As he walked around the edges of the scene from hell, he asked, "You came out and checked this, yourself?"

"Yep."

"And you didn't think to contact any of us?", Edward asked. He took his eyes off the scene long enough to look over at the sheriff who was on the opposite side of the display from him. To say he had a sheepish look on his face would be a dishonor to sheep. It was obvious he had made a judgement call as sheriff, one that is allowed by his office, but not the correct one. The look Lewis was giving his young replacement echoed that. This would probably create an abundance of false-alarm-type calls from Marcus in the future, but that was better than what could happen if he walked into a situation he couldn't handle.

"Are you seeing this, Father?", Edward asked.

"Yes."

The scene in front of them started with the bodies of six headless squirrels, hanging from strings tied up in the trees, down to about head height. The arrangement made a circle. Inside the circle, the ground had been cleared of all debris, and was immaculate. There wasn't a rock, leaf, weed, or blade of grass, anywhere. Just black dirt. Edward looked closer, and discovered how that feat was accomplished. It had been burnt.

What *was* inside the burnt circle was the most disturbing scene of all. The heads of the six squirrels were on six sticks. Each faced away from the center. The ground was stained in areas, and Edward's eyes followed the dark red stains, which he assumed was created by using the blood of the slain animals. The lines created a pentagram on the ground, with all but one stick at the points. The remaining stick, and posted head, were at the center.

"We need to destroy this, all of this!", Edward exclaimed, and he began kicking at the sticks.

"What are you doing?", asked Sheriff Thompson. His voice strained and confused.

"He is right. We have to destroy this abomination," said Father Murray.

Without waiting for permission, or any further objection, Lewis pulled out his pocketknife and began cutting down the hanging bodies. As each body hit the ground, he used his shoe to push it into a pile. Later, before they left, he used his knife to dig a makeshift grave and shoved them, and their heads, in and pushed the dirt over the top of them with his boot. Edward used his feet to kick dirt over the burnt area, covering the unholy shape on the ground.

Sarah stood and watched, a hand over her mouth the whole time.

The five of them walked out of the woods quietly, and much faster than they had walked in. Edward eventually passed Sheriff Thompson. He hoped he could remember the way back to their cars. He would have to chance it, he had to get away from that scene. As far away as he could. A cold black weight sat in the pit of his stomach, and it grew heavier with every moment they spent there. Everywhere else in the world, well, except in six other places, someone might dismiss this as misguided teens messing around, or following some example they saw in a movie or music video, if anyone still watched those. That was not the case here. He knew this was real. What whoever was messing with was as real as it gets. This would be like loading a gun and pulling the trigger, not expecting the bullet to fire, or lighting the fuse on a bomb, and not expecting it to explode, strictly out of some misguided belief. You knew damn well what you were doing in both instances. Whoever was doing this knew damn well what they were doing here too. Even if they didn't know the 'how' or 'why', they knew the 'what'. Not knowing the 'how' could be the most dangerous of all. They could stumble upon something dark and evil just as easily and summon it on purpose. That was the source of the dark weight. This was not something they could ignore.

He emerged out of the trees and marched toward the cars. When he reached them, he turned and waited for the others. Once the sheriff was close enough Edward demanded, "I need a map!"

"A what?", he asked in reply.

"I assume you have a map of the town in your car Marcus." Edward caught himself after he had said it, but didn't attempt to correct it and just let it sit out there in the air.

The sheriff popped the trunk and searched. He closed the trunk and walked around to the hood of his patrol car with a fan-folded map. His hands spread it flat on the hood, using the flashlight he had on his belt as a weight to hold one side down against the wind.

"Where are we?", asked Edward.

Lewis pointed to a spot on the map, his finger then moved a little off State Road 192. "That spot was right here."

"Where was Kevin found?", Edward asked.

"Harper Hill Road, about two miles past Walter's Creek, over here," the sheriff said, and he pointed to the spot on the map again.

Edward's eyes scanned the area between the two spots. It was a constant span of woods, not a single crossroad or house. There was an old logging road, still noted on the map, that cut into the woods about a quarter of a mile, but that was it. He then looked out further, along that same line of woods, until to the north it ran into a very familiar spot, and he placed his finger on the ball field.

"This isn't just a coincidence," he said.

12

The storm cleared, leaving devastation behind. Wind-whipped debris was scattered everywhere, as a quiet relief settled over the survivors like a blanket, but it only stayed there for a moment. The grief of what was ahead of them wiped away that respite with a slap of reality. It was a seasonal storm. One that Sarah knew exactly how to handle. It was finally homecoming, and over the past three hours, every girl between the age of fifteen and eighteen in Miller's Crossing had led a reluctant parent through the doors of Myrtle's. Each parent that entered knew what was in store for them. Their daughter would try on no less than eight dresses, most that looked very similar to each other. After each dress was on, they would complain about the fit, and then finally select one that someone else just bought the last one in their size.

Once the madness cleared, the dresses that had been shoved on and off for the last few hours were miraculously still in one piece, but discarded all over the floor, along with a rain of sequins. A single run by the vacuum cleaner would take care of that before closing, but first she needed to rehang all the dresses. To her pleasure, Charlotte had stopped by to watch the madness, a madness that she would suffer through in another fifteen years. For now, it was just a spectator sport to her, and she was kind enough to stay behind to help Sarah and her part-time clerk, Judy Spencer, clean up the mess.

Judy was a high-school junior, herself, and daughter of the town's Chamber of Commerce president of the last twenty years. Before that, there wasn't a chamber, or a Tourism Department, either, which her father was also in charge of. During a town council meeting in the mid-1980s, Walter Spencer laid out a plan to put Miller's Crossing on the map. It involved setting up a Chamber of Commerce and Tourism Office. Both of which he had to explain what they were to the council. Neither was the only topic he had had to explain to the council. There was a great debate around whether they wanted to put Miller's Crossing on the map. Most of the residents enjoyed being the little secret that no one knew about. Mostly because of the secret they all hid. Walter was persistent and, after several meetings, they agreed. They would establish both and name him president of each, but they diverted no public funding to either. That didn't stop him from putting a square of wood, with both department names on it, in front of their home, nor buying a nice new suit and a bow tie that he wore every day as he walked around greeting the same people over and over, with a cheap thousand-dollar smile. There was a rumor that had spread through whispers, that had resonated in every corner of the town, that his desire to put their sleepy home on the map, seemed to coincide with his realtor's license. No one could ever be sure.

His daughter, much like her father, saw an opportunity and took steps to grab it. She was a little better at it than he was. Judy had had her eye on a dress for weeks. A blue chiffon dress that stopped just above her knees, with a single row of silver beading around the waist. She knew what was coming and, wisely, had purchased it before the store opened, with Sarah's permission and then hid it in the back. Now she had it on and twirled and danced in front of the wall of full-length mirrors in the changing room, while Sarah worked her way from the front of the store to the back, folding the entire way. Charlotte flanked her, moving up the right side, doing the same thing. In an hour, maybe a few minutes more, they would have it all cleaned up and, if they were lucky, Judy might come out to help with the last few articles of clothes.

"Stop it," Sarah chastised her friend.

"I am serious. With the way they talk about you, I feel I should lay palm fronds down to line your path." Charlotte grabbed a green dress that was puddled on the floor and rushed around a display to lay it flat on the floor in front of Sarah. "Your majesty," she gushed, the last syllable of which was a giggle as a balled up t-shirt hit her upside the head.

"Look. I know that has everyone freaked out but I, nor my father, have done anything yet. We probably won't need to. The sheriff is trying to find who did it."

The "that" she talked about was the satanic display found in the woods five days ago. Even though they had all agreed to keep it quiet, the whole town was talking and speculating about it by Tuesday. With all the weirdness that happened here, this was a first, and it made everyone uneasy. Something that, before now, seemed to not be possible in this community.

"Marcus?", laughed Charlotte. "Please. He couldn't find them if they paraded down the road in front of his car wearing an upside down cross, with black flames shooting from their hands. We need you."

"No, you don't. This is a matter for the cops," said Sarah, who kept on folding and hanging up dresses without missing a beat.

"Sarah Meyer, that sounds like your father talking. Since you got back you have been running around town like a warrior, but now you take a step back. You have an obligation to this community. To the people who look at you like a savior."

"Jesus Christ, Charlotte," Sarah exclaimed with her back to her friend. Her hands had stopped folding and hanging clothes for the first time in the last twenty minutes. They sat, still holding a yellow silk dress that hung loosely in her grip. The long flowing skirt fluttered slightly in the air, moving through a vent in a nearby wall. "I am not Jesus, or God hims..." A loud slam and the tinkle of a little bell cut off Sarah. Both women jumped and spun around. Sarah's heart beat in her throat.

"Oh, dear me. We didn't mean to slam the door," said Eileen Connors. "The wind outside.... Well..." The late-thirties former homecoming queen stood in the door with the same surprised look on her face as Sarah and Charlotte. Her daughter, Lindsey, stood behind her and peered over her shoulder at the scene as the silence descended even deeper, going from uncomfortable to awkward. It stopped short of damaging, thanks to Eileen. "Everything all right? Are we too late? Lindsey here needs a dress."

"Not at all," Sarah said as she put down the dress she was folding and hastily moved toward the door. Her eyes cut in Charlotte's direction as she passed. She extended her hand toward Lindsey, who shied away from taking it for a few seconds, before finally accepting. "There are plenty still left, might take a bit to find it in all of this, but we will take our time to find you the perfect gown."

Lindsey was the opposite of her mother in every way. Not that she was not pretty. She was gorgeous. Red hair, blue eyes, corrected perfect smile, and just the hint of freckles to give her lily-white complexion a hint of character and glow. A picture of Americana. The 'girl next door' with that little something extra, but she was quiet. Not at all the outgoing person her mother is. To be fair, many felt she didn't have any other choice than to become a shriveled flower under the shadow cast by her mother. Her mother was the former homecoming queen, Miss Crooked Road 1997 and, as she always reminded everyone, 11th runner up to Miss Virginia 1998. She never explained to anyone how she figured out she was the 11th runner up. Only the top three are ever revealed, but few questioned her, or her stature as a local celebrity. Only her personality was larger than her stardom. She lit up a room when she walked in. Even if it was full of doom and gloom, as the shop headed toward, she pulled it out of the depths of despair. It was said around town to never have a funeral without inviting her.

For the moment, with the shop all to herself, Sarah treated Lindsey like a beauty queen, and helped her find the perfect dress. They perused the racks, and the random dresses still scattered on the floor. There was a slight murmur at the front of the store, where Charlotte and Eileen, a woman old enough to be their own mother, gossiped like two old hens at Ruthie's Perm and Clip. Sarah ignored them and kept her attention on the young girl. Well, mostly, one eye kept looking over at the two, and couldn't help but notice how they seemed to look in her direction most of the time. The volume and intensity of their gossip spilled over in her direction, causing a ball of tension to build inside of her, and it swelled and pulsate in her core.

With five dresses selected, Sarah set Lindsey up in a dressing room and then found a comfortable spot to lean against on the opposite wall, while she waited. Eileen joined her to wait and help provide her judgement on each dress, which was the only one that counted. The gossip didn't stop, it only changed locations, which now allowed Sarah to hear what they were talking about. At first, she stayed quiet and let the two keep going. This wasn't the first time, and would not be the last time, but this was different. Maybe it was the conversation Eileen and her daughter walked in on that had started the little ball of tension in the pit of Sarah's stomach, and hearing the murmur from them, with the looks in her direction gave it the power to grow. Now hearing what, exactly, they were talking about sent it bouncing up and down at a furious pace. Each bounce sent it closer to escaping up and out of her mouth. The last bounce broke out and she said, "That's enough, you two. You know I am standing right here."

Both stopped and their mouths clamped shut as they stood there, stunned. Sarah looked straight ahead at the dressing room door. "My family are people just like you, and everyone else in this town," she said.

There was no immediate reply from any of them, sending the shop into an uncomfortable silence for the second time in an hour. Just like the first one, they were saved by the opening of a door. The look on Lindsey's face said it all as she walked out in a white knee-length dress, with simple pearl beads sown in to give color and texture. Not a word was spoken by the three women as the girl turned in front of the mirror while biting her lip. Her eyes searched her reflection for anything that would change her mind, but nothing did, and it was obvious when she turned around toward the others. Her mother held out a single thumbs down, sending her daughter back into the dressing room to try on her next selection. Lindsey didn't protest, instead, she provided an affirmation, "I should have known not to select a white one." The door clicked closed.

"Sorry, Sarah," said Eileen. "It is hard for those of us that have been here for a while, and heard all the stories, not to look at your family like some kind of savior. Times were dark while your family was gone. Now, with this abomination found in the woods, everyone will be looking for you guys more."

"I get that, just don't expect too much. We are human and people just like you."

"Fair enough," she said.

"And you, don't go around spreading any kind of stories, please?", Sarah asked Charlotte, who just nodded.

"What do you think it means?"

"What do you mean?"

"That display you all found. What does it mean?", asked Eileen.

"I don't know. Most likely nothing," replied Sarah.

"Wendall Lockridge said he heard it was done by a hunter who wanted to summon a demon to help him hunt."

Sarah laughed and said, "You tell Wendall if he tries to do that, chances are the demon will hunt him."

"Jen Frye, over on Randolph Street said she heard it was a bunch of bored teens repeating something they saw in a movie," said Charlotte.

"That is probably closer to the truth than any of the other guesses I have heard over the last few days. Maybe I should tell my dad to assign more homework to solve the boredom problem."

A panicked response of "Please don't," exploded out of the dressing room, creating a moment of shared laughter among the three women.

"All I know is, we all feel better with you and your father around. You guys will keep us safe."

Sarah felt an inexplicable feeling of illness at that statement that caught her off guard. It had the taste of repulsiveness, mixed with hatred, as it climbed up her throat, but never emerged higher. A few quick swallows ensured it returned down from where it came. What had caused it was still a mystery as she said, "We will try."

Sarah was considering the possibility of the stress of that responsibility as Lindsey emerged in a low-cut, pink, form-fitting number. The smile on the girl's face told the rest what her thoughts of the dress were. Too bad, she had only made it out of the room a few feet before her mother said, "Absolutely not! Might as well just walk around with your boobs out in the open. Go back and change." Lindsey turned and stomped back in. The door slammed against its own lock and bounced back into the teen, much to the amusement of her mother.

"You must think we are all silly. You and your father have skills and abilities. There is no chance anyone who doesn't know what they are doing can really cause any trouble."

Sarah nodded her head and said, "Very true," in the best reassuring-sounding voice she could muster. The whole time, her eyes were focused on Charlotte, who had a very nervous look on her face.

13

"People believe in that stuff?", Jacob asked his father. He rarely took an interest in whatever his father was doing when he was camped at the dining room table amidst stacks of papers and books. What pre-teen and now teenage boy would take an interest in the grading of papers on Henry David Thoreau? There are cool jobs for a parent to have, and there is teaching. Jacob had adjusted to it a little better than Sarah had. His cool, what Jacob called a hobby, didn't hurt.

"Some," said his father, from behind the stack of books. This was more of his light reading on demonology and the darker subjects. Something he had looked into before but, thanks to the events of last weekend, he had found a renewed interest in. "People believe in a range of religions. Your Western Civilization class covered that, I believe."

"Yeah, but this?"

"Yeah, this. Religion is just a set of beliefs one holds so dear they worship and put above themselves. There are hundreds of them around the world. This one is no different. It just carries a stigma that most of the world either look down on or fear. When you really look at it, cannibalism and head-shrinking are forms of religion. What is sacred and acceptable to some, might disgust to others."

Jacob said, "I guess." He remembered covering the most popular forms of religion during Mr. Macey's World History class last year, and he made a similar point to what his father had. It was foreign to his brain to consider Satanic rituals the same as Communion in church. Time, and he guessed experience, was what was needed to get to the place his father was on this topic. So far, his father had shared a little of that side of the world with him, but had yet to go too in depth, or take him along when he and Father Murray headed out to handle a situation.

Not that he hadn't asked. He had, almost every time they left, since he was thirteen. Well, except that month or so stretch during the summer two years ago. Jacob had his first full-on experience that summer. He knew he had felt them a little for years before, but nothing like this. The times before were just the feeling that something was there, or something was watching him. A feeling most people might just chalk up to getting the creeps, but something deep inside of him knew differently. Then, a late evening in June, while the last rays of sunlight still illuminated the horizon, he felt a cold chill down his spine, followed by the sensation of hundreds of needles plunging into his skin. While his body had processed those feelings, his mind struggled with the presence, or lack thereof, it felt. There was something there, but not at the same time, it was more like a void. A big dark hole, and the emptiness, brought a fear he hadn't felt before. It took him several weeks before he told his father about the incident, which prompted the second father-son talk they had. The first being about the birds and the bees. The second, about spirits and demons, was the easier of the two for Edward.

Jacob leaned back in a chair, opposite his father, at the dining room table. His attention was focused on the pages of the book he flipped through, which was just the latest of the books his father had moved from the 'to be read' pile and to the 'looked through' pile. The pages were full of satanic and occult symbology. Some were obvious, such as the upside-down cross and the pentagram, but seeing some of the symbols, such as the pyramid and all-seeing eye, which is labeled as the Eye of Horus in the book, was rather surprising to him. *"What is an occult symbol doing on our dollar bills?"*, he asked himself. His eyes continued to scan the page, and found other, similar, common symbols and then noticed a link. At least at the symbolic level. Common symbols, just oriented differently, have a new meaning in the world of the occult. He thought about this on a deeper level and understood how that would make it easy to hide occult references in common sight. To one person, the symbol meant one thing, but something different to others.

"Dad, there is a dark presence in the house," announced Jacob.

Edward's head shot up from his study, but relaxed when he heard the door slam.

"It's getting closer, and it is really evil," said Jacob.

"Funny, squirt," Sarah said, with a slap to the back of his head. She reached over and grabbed the book he was reading. "Interesting school assignment. I don't remember a class on the Occult when I was in school."

"Just doing some research. Father Murray is doing some of the same," Edward said.

"Dad, symbols are just a tool. It is the intent of the person using it that worries me," Sarah said.

Her father just nodded.

"Anyway, I am exhausted. Took forever to clean up the store. I am going to take a shower and relax."

Edward looked at his phone and then asked, "I didn't realize it was so late. What about dinner?"

"Already ate. Actually, I let Judy close up so I could grab some takeout for Kevin, and ate with him."

"How is he doing?", asked Edward. He placed the book he was looking through on the top of the pile to his right. Jacob, spying an opportunity to snag another book, grabbed it, and was now flipping through it. He was not sure if his father was done with it, but he had put it down, and that made it fair game in his book.

"Okay, I guess. There are times he doesn't seem to be himself. Still doesn't remember what happened to him."

"Dang. I still can't shake the feeling this is all related. I would like to talk to him again, when he is ready."

"Well," Sarah started using a tone that usually meant she was asking permission for something that normally would be refused. Jacob made a habit of mocking this tone every chance he could get, and then reveled in their father's refusal of whatever she was asking for, but not this time. His focus was on the book, but his ears were listening to the surrounding conversation.

"He could come over for dinner. He hasn't left his parents' house since he got out of the hospital Monday afternoon. They won't let him. I am sure they would be okay if he was coming over here."

Edward eagerly agreed, "Okay."

"Tomorrow?" Sarah asked before her father completed his reply.

"Not sure tomorrow will be good. Tomorrow is the homecoming dance. I have to chaperone, and your brother will be there. How about Sunday?"

"Tomorrow is fine, we don't need you there," Jacob said. His eyes looked at his father over the top of the book he was reading.

"Nonsense," Edward said. "It's my job." A wide smile garnished his face.

Jacob's eyes dropped back to the page. He didn't think his father would go for it, but had seen the opportunity and tried. Not that it bothered him if he was there or not.

"Okay, Sunday," Sarah agreed, reluctantly.

"Great. I will see if the father can come, too," Edward said.

"A priest... witnesses... family.. we can get them hitched before dessert," Jacob said, drawing another slap on top of his head from his sister.

14

Jacob may handle being a student at the same school as his father better than Sarah had, but that didn't mean it was something he was "cool" with in all situations. There was a hierarchy of tolerance. Sarah had it too, but the reactions that went with each tier were less severe with Jacob.

School was the first level. The avoidance Edward experienced from his daughter was replaced by the open recognition, and the occasional high-five, as he passed his son and his friends in the hall.

School events, such as football games, were level two. The group of friends all gathered around Edward, cheering and talking sports, was a departure from the avoidance of the leper he saw from his daughter. That might be a guy thing. Age and parental status seem to disappear between guys at a sporting event. Either only appear during the discussion of the various principles of the game. Most Jacob's friends are always calling for their team to pass the ball. An influence from the video game age. Unless you had a rare talent at quarterback, a solid running game was the most likely path to success at the high school level. A fact that never seemed to sink in with the younger generation, even after a disappointing loss.

The last level, and the one with the most penal reaction, was at different school events, school social events. Exhibit A, the homecoming dance. A place where parents were not only not desired, but not allowed. Hundreds of sets of eyes roll, and thousands of sighs exhale out, contributing to the level of greenhouse gases in the environment, as they tolerated parents for that ever-treasured photo of their children, and their date, all dressed up. Several die second deaths if the parents mess up the first photo and have to take a second. That is where it ended for most. Unless your parent was a teacher who had to chaperone. The torture continued throughout the night. Sometimes ground rules were put in place, which was the case in the Meyer household. When Sarah went to the homecoming dance her senior year, there was a list ten rules long. Jacob went simple, he was always the simpler child, those rules were: I won't embarrass you. You won't embarrass me. They seemed mutually agreeable, which is why Edward stayed away from the balloon-arched entryway until Jacob and his date entered.

It wasn't hard to spot them upon entry. Jacob was one of the taller students at the school, but that wasn't what caused him to stand out this time. The turquoise and hot pink paisley print bowtie and cummerbund he had ordered online picked up stray beams from the various black lights positioned around the gym. The visual effect was not intentional. Neither was his attempt to be flamboyant. A word that should never be used to describe Jacob. His date, Molly Webster, was indecisive about her dress and changed every other day. Something her mother indulged by buying both of the dresses she had liked. To make sure they matched, Jacob ordered a bowtie and cummerbund set that contained both colors.

For the entire evening, Edward, and an army of twenty teachers, walked around the outer ring of the gym, monitoring what happened inside their ring. Nothing was added to the punch bowl to give it a bit more punch. It seemed to just be a fixture from tradition, and not a source of refreshment anyway. The attendees opted for soft drinks, or just water, more often than anyone ladled up the sweet red syrup. The six-inch rule given birth to in the forties was just the talk of legend, not one anyone enforced. Only if there was some excessive bump and grind action going on would there be a polite tap on the shoulder, but that would be it.

The music pounded for hours on end. Edward took a few breaks and walked outside, or into one of the adjoining hallways. The thump of the bass was still audible below the ringing that would last for hours after the dance ended. Even when the music was turned off to announce the homecoming court, there was a constant ring, and a subconscious thump of bass. With the court crowned, and no pig's blood raining down from above, the music kicked up again, the dancing resumed, as did the duties of the chaperones.

"I never went to homecoming," Cheryl Avery leaned in and said over the sound of the music. The sophomore English teacher grew up in Miller's Crossing and had attended this very high school. "It was my bad luck, always had strep throat. Every single year."

"Wow," said Edward.

"Yeah, the doc thought it might have been fall allergies that started it."

Edward felt he needed to share a story, but couldn't share the truth. To this day, only three people in town knew the truth of where he was during his high school years. This was neither the time nor the place to share, *"I didn't either. I was in a mental hospital. Not allergy related."* Still feeling the need to share he said, "I don't remember much about the dances, but the homecoming games I do."

"What are you guys talking about?", asked Mark Grier, who was passing by on one of his hundred or more loops he had made around the gym that night.

"Reminiscing about our homecomings," Cheryl said.

"Well, I can say nothing we did is going on here tonight. Not a single person has tried to empty a flask into the punch bowl. Something I did twice in one year, I might add. We have found no couples in any of the dark corners that I remember from when I was a student. Seems kind of boring to me."

"I like it that way," said Edward.

Mark slapped him on the shoulder and said, "You would, old friend." Then he resumed his patrol for the night. He was one of the few that was still walking around. The night was winding down, and there was not much the chaperones had to handle during the night. A few even joined the students out on the dance floor. Something Edward had considered, but knew it would break the second of his and Jacob's two rules. So, he stood back with the other teachers and enjoyed the music as they watched a few of their colleagues attempt to reclaim their youth. The concerns of the past week were gone from Edward's mind. No images of animal heads on sticks, or pentagrams drawn in blood. Just a slice of small town America. Happiness, and the cold prick of a needle.

Edward's head whipped around the room. He saw nothing but the happy scene he had seen just moments ago. There was another needle prick, and another frantic search around, but still, nothing. Not what he expected. When the chill hit him, he looked again, and this time looked above him and caught sight of an air conditioner vent above his head. He felt a little silly, and brushed it off to being tired, the dark lighting, and the loud music.

A bloodcurdling scream rammed through the entry and into the gym, freezing those dancing. The music continued, but no one moved. Then a few teachers hurried in the door's direction. Edward took a step forward, watched, and waited. The next sight he saw at the door sent him into a full run across the dance floor, bouncing off students who didn't clear the way in time. Each step caused another pinprick, then another, and then another, until his entire spine tingled and crawled. Gooseflesh developed along the back of his neck by the time he reached Jacob, who stood at the door waving for him to hurry. Together they ran out the door that was choked off by students who stood around and gawked at the scene outside.

They pushed through into a scene that sent Edward flashing back to the football field, eight years ago. These were not ghosts, they were demons. Their bodies were a hellish cross of animals, humans, and something Edward's mind couldn't find a comparison for. Their screeches rattled the world to its core. They were poised on top of cars. With each step or stomp they took, the roofs bent or caved ominously low above the students trapped inside. The car windows muffled their screams, but the terror on their faces was visible through the clear glass.

One, larger than all the others, was positioned in the middle of the parking lot. Its placement, blocked any attempt to escape. Not that anyone had tried to drive with the others perched on top. You could run to safety, but no one in the cars or in the gym had made any attempt to escape. Fear, not the demons, trapped them.

Jacob moved toward one car, to help his friends. Edward screamed, "Jacob, no!" He stopped in his tracks as a demon hopped off the car and hissed at him. It then turned back to the car and put a single claw under it. With a simple move of its arm, it flipped the car over on its roof. Shards of blue safety glass from the windows and windshield scattered out, away from the car, letting out the screams of the teens as they rolled with the car and then landed in silence on the roof.

The larger one, with cloven hoofs and the disfigured upper body of a man, walked forward. Its gait was smooth and rhythmic, but his arm movements were gangly and awkward. Both arms were different lengths and sizes. Its head had facial features, but none of them were in the correct place, or correct size. One eye was bigger than the other. The mouth didn't fit the face at all. To Edward it looked like it was made of the various parts of different people. That also explained the sound it made when it looked up and screamed. It wasn't one or two voices. It was dozens. Each uttering a different command. Each targeted to one other, who subserviently obeyed and began ripping at the sheet metal of the car roofs they stood on.

"Stop!" yelled Edward, as he held up the cross he always carried neatly tucked in the pocket of the tweed jacket, that he wore everywhere.

Each did as he commanded and turned their attention to him. It was times like this, Edward wished he had thought things through before he took action. He had done this before, but that was just with a single spirit. Easier to handle, and no need to back down. There was a portion of him that feared for his life at this moment, and he felt his weight rock backward as his gave ground to them. A lesson Father Murray had told him once, and then was reaffirmed by Sarah, yelled back at him, and he took a step forward, and then another. A slight glow began in the center of the cross and traversed out the crossbar. Inside, Edward prayed a deep prayer. This wasn't one from the book. The book was still tucked in his pocket. It wasn't one he had memorized from the book, or anything similar to any of the ones his father, grandfather, or any other Meyer had ever used. It was his own. His own approach and spin. Something he had come up with thanks to the guidance he had received from Father Lucian, and his own experimenting. The words had yet to be written in the book. At least he hadn't written it word for word. He didn't need to. It would mislead the next holder of this responsibility. There was an addition to the book. A single blank page now had three words written on it: "Empower Your Faith!" At that moment, Edward was reciting a personal prayer to empower his own faith.

With every word he whispered, the glow became brighter. His eyes stayed locked on the creature in the parking lot. The others were not his concern, not yet. They obeyed this creature, and this creature was who he dealt with.

Edward broke his prayer and ordered, "Jacob, get back to the gym!"

"But, Dad!"

"No buts..." Edward interrupted. He needed to remove his son from harm's way before what was next. He would have to get closer to the creature and make contact with it. That was what his one and only encounter with a demonic presence had taught him. He hoped the light froze them, like before, which would make it easier, but it hadn't. The creature moved forward, curious of the cross, not afraid.

"Demon, you are not permitted here. Our Lord and Savior Jesus Christ gave his life for the forgiveness of our sins, not yours. You are a vile creature that is not allowed in the realm of our lord."

If Edward had to list the 100 different reactions he expected, what happened wouldn't even come close to making that list. The dozens of voices that had barked orders moments before seemed to laugh, not from the creature, but from above. Then it turned and jumped a hundred yards away, followed by the others. Another jump sent them into the tree line. Their screams and screeches faded to nothing but a distant echo.

The thump of the music continued behind Edward and several screams emerged as teens opened their car doors and fell out on the ground in hysterical masses of humanity.

15

The mood in the Meyer's house was as dark and dank as the weather outside. While the rain pelted the windows and side of the house, the details of the previous night beat on Edward's thoughts like the music from the dance. The wind whipped and howled outside. The screams of the teenagers replaced the dull ringing from a night of loud music. Lightning flashed and thunder boomed across the farmland. The car flipped over and over, all night long and throughout the day. Each time landing in a thunderous crunch of steel and glass.

Adding to it, not a person spoke to anyone throughout the day. All talking ceased after a brief conversation between Edward and Sarah, when she returned home after them. He explained to her what happened, wanting her feedback. Her interpretation. She was the only one of the three who was properly trained in these matters. It was something Edward would never admit openly, but he felt inferior to his daughter. It wasn't just because of the training she had. From the moment she had shown the ability, she was not only more capable, but she handled it better. There was a quiet confidence and calm that exuded from her, even in the most stressful of situations. Not a bead of sweat, or moment of tension in her voice. She was calm and cool. That was where he felt inferior. He had years on her in experience, in both life and his spiritual involvements. His past life was anything but smooth, which he always felt prepared him to handle the little bumps that appeared in the grand plan of his life. Even though some events still got to him. Still pushed his stress level to a point of distraction and self-doubt. Both were dangerous at the wrong time.

The events of the night rattled him. His story rambled back and forth, and he often stopped mid-sentence to back up and add a detail to something he had said minutes earlier. The speed of Edward's words picked up as the stress level in him increased, but he was the only one. The tone, speed, and meaning of his daughter's words remained calm and consistent, even when she corrected him. He finished recalling the details, in as vivid and lifelike detail as he could. Even his heart believed the retelling and pounded inside his chest. He sat and watched his daughter for a reaction. She had none. Was she even listening to him? Did she not hear him tell her about the demons, and the flipping of the car? What about how they reacted, or didn't react, to his presence? He wanted her take on things, her trained impression. Why wasn't she saying anything? These were the questions that bounced around inside his head during what he felt was the minutes or longer since he had finished telling her. It only seemed that way because of his excited state. Actually, it had been mere seconds.

Sarah broke her silence and asked, with the same calm demeanor Edward had become jealous of, "Nothing? They didn't move back, or act frightened of you at all?"

Confounded, Edward said, "Not even at the light."

Much to his disappointment, the rest of their conversation didn't shed any light. Nothing they taught her, or any of the cases she had studied, were like this. After half an hour, both reached the same conclusion. This was something new. To Edward, it was new and troubling.

With all the distractions rolling in his head, he had a long day of cleaning, and then cooking to prepare for a dinner that was also new and troubling. His daughter, his princess, was bringing over a guy to meet the family. This had never happened before, and Edward didn't know how to react. Should he be friendly, be the over-protective parent and sit and leer at him in judgement, or maybe study every movement the young man made?

Other than television, which he hated to admit inspired certain aspects of his parenting, his only experience in this matter was from the vantage point of the young man. Karen's father had him under a microscope from the moment he entered. The handshake lasted a little longer than Edward was comfortable with. Edward was never sure why, but human contact was something he always found uncomfortable. Without a logical explanation, he chalked it up to his years in the hospital, with the only contact occurring when blood samples were needed. This time there was a slight tightening of pressure in the grip, as if to check his. He remembered his father once saying you could tell a lot about a man by his handshake. Karen's father was trying to get the entire report out of this one. For the rest of the evening, Edward felt his eyes on him. A fact that was reinforced every time Edward looked at him. That sensation has a way of unnerving even the most confident person, not that Edward was. He became subconscious about how he chewed, placed his hands on the table, gripped his fork and, worst of all, looked at Karen. Each time he glanced in her direction he thought he heard the gruff voice of her father say, *"Keep your lust-filled eyes off of my baby girl."*

The appearance of a spectral visitor behind Karen's mother while they sat at the table drinking coffee was absolutely the worst timing he had ever experienced. Edward had to fight every instinct inside him to not look at it for longer than just a glance. There was no predicting how her father would interrupt him staring off into space. *Karen, is your date on drugs or something?* Her father was not physically intimidating. He was actually smaller in stature than Edward, balding, wore glasses, and talked with a bit of a lisp. It was his role in that engagement that created the tension.

Edward could only predict that it would be the same tonight. Kevin Stierers was a young man he was familiar with. Only seven years ago, he was a student in his class. A well-mannered boy, with a lot of pride in his schoolwork. Something Edward could tell right away. English and literature were not subjects that had an abundance of tutoring or after class requests. Not like math and science, where someone might misunderstand a formula or theorem, which can easily be corrected. They were objective. Edward's subjects were more subjective. Especially when he taught creative writing. Which made it even more curious when students stayed behind for questions. The names of those students stuck with him. Kevin was one. He had received a C- on a creative writing project. It was a 5,000 word story, on the topic of their choice. Upon receiving the paper back, Kevin stayed after class to understand the source of the grade. Edward explained, he could tell all the different breaks Kevin took while writing it. The voice changed during each. So, for an hour after school that day, they discussed the story and how it could have been written in each of the different voices.

The good impression he had of Kevin helped, but didn't change that this would be a new role, a new interaction, and it had been several years since he had last spoke to the young man, other than just a hello in passing in town. Edward also knew, while he needed to be protective of Sarah, he couldn't take it too far. He wanted Kevin to be comfortable. There was still what had happened to him that night that Edward wanted to discuss and find out more about.

The distractions in his head only led to a few mistakes while cleaning, and one while cooking, when a pot boiled over while on the stove. Both of which drew a minor explosion inside. Each time Sarah pitched in to help pick up the bag of trash he dropped, or grab the pot, while Edward kept preparing the roast. She was as calm as a cucumber.

At a quarter after seven, there was a knock on the door. The doorbell hadn't worked since Edward was a child. Edward walked out of the kitchen to answer the door, but Sarah sprinted down the stairs past him. She looked nice. This was not the half cut-off shirt and shorts that matched the definition of the word that she usually wore when going out. This was a long flowing skirt, a white cardigan sweater which Edward didn't know she owned, and flats. No boots with heels. No three inch or higher heels. His heart fluttered for a moment as she looked and moved liker her mother, minus the dark hair that she got from her father.

"Be nice," she warned both her father, standing in the kitchen's door, and Jacob, who sat on the sofa watching television.

She opened the door, and a scene out of the 1950s strolled in. Kevin, dressed in his Sunday best suit and tie, stood there with flowers in his hand. The only thing missing was a black and white hue to it, and a toothy grin on Kevin as he greeted him with a very sappy, "Good evening, Mr. Meyer." Instead, Kevin walked in and gave Sarah the flowers and a hug. Then he walked forward and extended his hand to Edward, who still stood in the doorway to the kitchen, with a dishrag in one hand.

"Hi, Mr. Meyer," Kevin said.

Edward took his hand, "Hi, Kevin. It's good to see you." The handshake was firm and confident. A good start.

"I probably look a lot different than when you last saw me?", asked Kevin.

That he did, but Edward didn't know how to respond, and must have looked as confused on the outside as he felt on the inside.

"I mean in the hospital. My family and I are thankful that you and Father Murray came and checked on me."

"Glad you are feeling better Kevin," Edward said, with a bit of relief. Kevin was not responsive when they had visited him. He was not sure if Kevin had even realized they were there. There was a chance he was talking about the change in appearance since high school. The longer haired, t-shirt wearing student was now the suit-wearing man standing in his living room, holding his daughter's hand.

"I still have a few things to finish up for dinner. Make yourself at home," Edward said.

"Thank you, sir."

Before walking back into the kitchen, Edward offered, "Can I get you a drink or something? Some soda, water, maybe coffee?"

"No, sir, I am good."

Edward pushed through the door to the kitchen, leaving them in the living room. Behind him, he heard Sarah and Kevin talking and then heard, "Heya Jake, nice game. I played a bit of fall league myself."

The four of them enjoyed a dinner that didn't stretch Edward's rather limited culinary abilities. A roast that basically cooked itself once the oven was set, with rice and vegetables that only required him to boil water. During the meal, Edward tried not to put too much of a spotlight on their guest. Conversation took to normal topics, such as his job at the local mill. Remember when's; talking about people and events from when he was in Edward's class, and sports. A given topic when there are three males sitting around a table, much to Sarah's dislike. Sarah's dislike appeared more than Edward would have expected, and it didn't go unnoticed by Kevin. To say there was an odd vibe between the two of them would be a fair description.

Simple questions such as, "So, Kevin, how long have you been at the mill?" Something any father would ask, with no ulterior motives behind it, other than making sure he could be a good provider for his baby. This simple question didn't draw a look of embarrassment, or any daggers from daughter aimed at the father. Instead, there was a visible look of stun, followed by a pause from Kevin, before he looked at Sarah for, what appeared to be affirmation or permission, before answering. That happened after every question. The deeper or more probing the question was, the more Kevin looked uncomfortable. He looked down at his lap, and then at Sarah.

When Edward asked how they met, Kevin stared down at his lap, biting his bottom lip to the point of discoloration. There was a single long exhale before he looked at Sarah with a pained expression. Their eyes met, and his mouth opened, but nothing came out. Sarah immediately jumped in and said, "It was just a random meeting two months ago. We hadn't seen each other since school and bumped into each other. I was closing up the boutique when he was walking by."

"Wow, that is a chance meeting. Didn't think anything like that could happen. Seems you bump into everyone at least once a month around here."

They shared another look. Sarah's pained and uncomfortable. Kevin's was a complete lack of confidence. "I know. I was so busy at the mill, I didn't make it to town much," Kevin said and then took a long sip of his iced tea.

As the conversation returned to topics that were less contentious, the visible level of discomfort and anxiety reduced in their guest. It melted away completely when he and Jacob engaged in a discussion about baseball, both their playing days and favorite professionals. Edward took that moment to clear the table and take the spotlight off of Kevin for a few moments. Sarah helped her father.

It was on the second trip into the kitchen when Edward asked, "Is Kevin feeling all right?"

"Yes, why?", Sarah asked, annoyed, while she scraped a plate into the trash can.

"He just seems uncomfortable."

Sarah finished rinsing off the dish and placed it in the sink. She walked to the kitchen door and pushed it open. The sound of two people in a very lively debate, filled with laughter, leaked through into the kitchen. "He seems comfortable to me." She released the door, letting it swing shut.

"Yeah, now. But not earlier when we were talking."

Over the sound of running water as Sarah rinsed the remaining plates, she explained, "Come on Dad. It is because of you. Guys are nervous when they meet their girlfriend's father. I am sure you were nervous when you met Grandpa."

Edward was nervous, but not to the level he had just seen. It could just be that, or maybe that combined with what Kevin had been through just over a week ago. That could explain it, but Edward couldn't shake the feeling Kevin wasn't being honest. His mind lingered there, doing what it does best and worst. They say your brain has two sides, a logical and a creative. One side is usually stronger than the other. Most would think, with Edward's affinity for reading, the creative would be strongest, but he was quite the opposite. He had a very strong logical side, that tried to search for explanations. The equally strong creative side always participated, resulting in some rather interesting roller coaster rides that threatened to defy logic. At this moment, his logical and creative sides were struggling to balance each other out as they formulated what might be the truth about how they met. A truth that a father might not approve of. Maybe a friend's party, where the drinking got a little out of hand, and things went a little... Edward stopped his mind from finishing that sentence. It was uncomfortable just thinking about it. He couldn't imagine how it would feel explaining that to the girl's father. In the same situation, he might come up with the same clichéd story.

16

Edward sat back down at the table with a cup of coffee. Something he had just become used to after dinner. He found it made him feel more relaxed. Not at all what you would think. To him, it was a sign that his addiction to caffeine was far stronger than he believed. Not that he would try to cut back anytime soon. Anyone that tried might have to pry his hand off his cup in the morning or in the evenings. Good luck to them if they tried.

The joyous conversation he walked in on continued for a few minutes after he sat down. He didn't try to contribute. There was no way he was as much of a baseball aficionado as Jacob was. That kid ate, slept, dreamt, and breathed baseball. Anything Edward would attempt to contribute here most likely would be wrong, leading to Jacob's embarrassment. Embarrassing one child tonight was enough. Even though there was something in Edward that liked the challenge.

The conversation volleyed back and forth between Jacob and Kevin until they ran out of topics. Kevin appeared to be much more comfortable than he had earlier. Each answer, question, and topic flowed freely. Never any attempt to check with Sarah before saying anything. Not that she could provide any affirmation on this topic, she knew less than Edward did. She spent her time at Jacob's games focused on her phone's screen.

That changed when the baseball chatter wound down, and the bottom of Edward's coffee cup appeared. There was a brief, and semi-awkward silence, signaling the end of the conversation. Edward took it as an opportunity to jump in with his own topic. One that was not nearly as lively as the prior, and guaranteed to be more uncomfortable. He asked Jacob to excuse them for a minute, telling him he wanted to talk to Kevin alone. The immature "oooo" he let out as he got up and left the table struck like a hot poker into his sister's side, but the sting didn't last long. That, or she just ignored it. She immediately asked, "Mind if I stay?" Edward saw no harm in that and agreed.

He leaned forward and rested both of his forearms on the table, with his hands cupping his coffee cup. He knew he needed to tread lightly on this topic. What happened was obviously traumatic to Kevin. Anyone with any common sense, that saw him that day in the hospital, would know that. They would also be surprised to see that same catatonic individual sitting there in front of him as if nothing ever happened. That tipped Edward's suspicion that there was more than just shock at play. That a presence, of some type, had draped that condition over Kevin. That same presence could pull it away just as quickly. What that presence was? That was the question Edward needed to know. With the proximity of where they found Kevin, and the other oddities, he would be a fool to not suspect a connection.

There was no easy way to start, so he just went for it. "Kevin, I want to ask you some questions about the other day in the woods, if that is okay?"

Edward waited for an answer. The confident and joyful young man, that had just been rambling on about baseball with Jacob moments ago, was gone. Replacing him was the sullen and shrinking person that now sat across the table. Even the color drained from his face. He looked over at Sarah and then down again. She reached over and grabbed his hand. Again, he looked at her, and she whispered, "It's okay. Just answer what you can." Edward could see she squeezed his hand as she did.

"Kevin, you don't have to. But if you can, it would help. I believe everything is related. The more I know, the more I can put things together. Do you understand?"

Kevin's eyes said no, but his mouth said, "Sure."

"What can you tell me about that night?"

Kevin sat there, with the appearance of being lost in thought, as he tried to remember. Sarah leaned in closer, as if to comfort him, as he went through a struggle both could sense. The twitches of his jaw, back and forth in rapid succession, told of his mind recalling the events of the evening in vivid detail. The detail was disturbing and took a toll. Lines formed and crinkled across his forehead. The speed of the jaw twitching increased. The eyes looked at no one and everyone, all at the same time. Muscles in his forearm jerked under the skin as he squeezed Sarah's hand and then released it. She squeezed back, and he glanced in her direction.

"Well, my car stopped for no reason. Which was strange. I had plenty of gas, and both the lights and radio were still on. I tried to call for help, but didn't have service on my phone, so I got out and started walking. I remember, coming across the bridge there at Walter's Creek, but that's it. I don't remember anything else until I got home from the hospital."

"When you were walking, did any cars pass you?", asked Edward.

"No," Kevin said, with a shake of the head, after looking at Sarah.

"Anyone else out walking?"

Again, another look at Sarah, and then a shake of the head.

"Did you fall, maybe down the embankment? That area along the bridge is pretty steep," Edward asked, knowing good and well he didn't fall down the embankment. He was reaching, trying to help Kevin remember what happened.

"No. I remember walking across the bridge, and a ways past."

"What is the last thing you remember at all that night? Even just a flash?", Edward asked, sounding half agitated. He caught himself and checked his body posture to appear friendlier. The attempt appeared halfhearted on the exterior. He had leaned back away from the table, but his posture still maintained a forward lean toward Kevin.

Again, he looked at Sarah before he answered. The answer he gave was not much of one, "Dark."

"Dark?", asked Edward.

"Dark and quiet," Kevin answered, this time without looking at Sarah first. This prompted a squeeze of his hand. He glanced in her direction and smiled. "It was quiet. Oddly quiet, Mr. Meyer. That is what I remember last. No wind. No crickets. Not even the sound of the creek, which wasn't that far behind me. And then..." he trailed off and then glanced at Sarah again.

"And then what Kevin?"

"I don't know," he said timidly, while looking down at the table. "I don't know. I don't remember anything until I woke up at home."

"Do you remember being in the hospital?"

"No sir. The bracelet on my right arm was the only thing that told me I was there for sure."

17

"So he survived?", Charlotte asked.

"Yep, he did," said Sarah after a healthy sip of red wine from her goblet.

"I remember when Dan came over to meet my family. That boy had sweat through his shirt before he got to the door. His hands were shaking so bad when he reached for my dad's, I thought he would miss."

Charlotte reached over to pour more wine in Sarah's goblet. They were sitting in her living room on the couch together doing their normal debrief after either of them went out on a date. Most of the time it was Charlotte dishing on the details over a glass or two of wine. These sessions changed when she married Dan three years ago. They still got together. They still shared plenty of wine, but the topics were different. Only recently did they return to their roots when Sarah started seeing Kevin.

"Not Kevin," Sarah said. She took another sip of her wine. "He was the perfect gentleman. Walked in, shook my father's hand. It was yes sir, all night long. Even talked with my brother. He handled everything great, even the inquisition by my father."

Charlotte gave her a questioning look.

"About what happened to him that night. My father thinks something spiritual attacked him."

"Wow," gasped Charlotte. "Makes sense. What do you think? You're the expert."

"Not sure. Anything is possible. Kevin remembers nothing from that night, so it is impossible to know for sure."

"It is amazing."

"What is? Stuff like that shouldn't amaze anyone around these parts anymore."

"No, you dork," giggled Charlotte. "His recovery. In just over a week he went from in a coma to meeting your father. Man, talk about both an amazing and traumatic week."

"He wasn't in a coma. Just not responsive, and yes... an amazing recovery."

"I know why," said Charlotte. The statement produced an immediate shocked reaction on Sarah's face. Maybe it was the giggle that accompanied it.

"You do?", asked Sarah. The look on her face changed from shocked to one that looked like she had smelled something sour. Her nose up turned and scrunched. Her eyes leered at her friend.

The reaction caught Charlotte off guard. She was trying to be humorous, but had elicited a reaction from her friend she had never seen before. Even through the years of ribbing each had given the other, never anything like this. Her original comment was setting up a joke, a joke she timidly said the punchline to, "You have him under your spell."

"What spell?", Sarah asked sternly.

Looking for an escape out of the uncomfortable moment, Charlotte considered her options. She could finish the joke and hope it landed well, change the subject, or with her foot knock something off the coffee table that sat in front of her and hope it woke Melissa in the other room to give her an out. Her daughter, Melissa, slept in the other room. It was nap time, and her mother kept her on a very strict schedule. It was good for both baby and mother. Her luck, she had the one baby in the world that could sleep through anything. The scheduled nap time was a time for her to get a few things done around the home, which included vacuuming. An activity that never woke her, even when she came close to the nursery door.

That left two options, but the stare from her friend eliminated the second option. There was no way she was going to be able to change the subject, that was clear. That left just one.

"You know. The spell all women cast over men. I know once I gave it up to Dan, that was it. That man would have walked over hot coals and through a lion's den for me." She attempted to cackle, like she remembered hearing Blanche Devereaux on reruns her mom watched of "The Golden Girls." Instead of sounding mature, it came out weak and airy.

There was an uncomfortable silence that hung in the air between the two friends. It lasted long enough for Charlotte to squirm on the sofa before running out of ways to fidget with her hands. What she wouldn't give at that moment for a stack of magazines to straighten on the table, or something to pick up. Her eyes listened for the sound of her daughter in the other room, but all she heard was that silence. She reached forward and poured a little more wine in her goblet. A goblet that was already two-thirds full. She tried an innocent, "Come on, you can tell me?"

To her, Sarah looked like perplexed and conflicted. Her hands jerked for her wine goblet, stopped, then reached again. The contact made was not smooth as she gripped the stem of the glass. It produced ripples in the red liquid.

Having never seen her friend like this, Charlotte took the off ramp in this conversation and apologized, "Sorry. You know me. No topic is off limits."

"It's okay. It's not that," Sarah said.

"What is it? You know you can talk to me about anything Sarah."

"No, I mean I don't have him under that kind of spell."

"Not yet," added Charlotte.

18

"Father, are you around?" Edward bellowed. His call echoed among the rafters of the empty church's cathedral ceiling. Hearing his own voice in front and behind him was off putting. The same with hearing footsteps coming at him from all directions, knowing that he was the only one walking. It was enough to produce a little gooseflesh, even in these well-lit surroundings. He thought he was just being silly, but each time he looked around and caught a scene from one of the oddly different stained-glass windows, that was enough to send his skin crawling again. The next sound made him jump and squeal like a little girl.

"Over here, Edward."

The squeal echoed slightly as Edward composed himself and walked up to the front of the church, and then off to the right vestibule. Seated in a chair, with a rag in one hand and a silver dish in another, was Father Murray. Rubber gloves adorned both hands. The rag whipped around in a furious motion against the silver dish. A few swipes made a squeaking sound as the rag moved across the polished metal.

"What are you doing?", Edward said curiously, drawing out the "are".

"I can cleanse the soul with a prayer, but it takes elbow grease to clean the house of our Lord," he answered with a chuckle. "Once a week I sit down and polish all the silver to keep it looking nice. No fingerprints, see?", he asked, as he held the dish up for Edward to see before putting it down next to him and picking up one of several chalices that sat on the ground next to him. "What brings you by so early on a non-service day?"

"Had a conversation with young Kevin," Edward said.

"Ah, the dinner. I assume he survived dinner?"

"I think so. He walked out on his own two feet. Sarah was on pins and needles all night."

Father Murray's eyes and hands focused on the chalice, which had begun to shine, but his ears were listening, and he giggled at Edward's response. "I bet."

"He doesn't remember anything from that night, though. His car stopped for no reason, and he said his cell phone didn't have a signal."

Father Murray's hands stopped. One hand still held the chalice, and the other pressed the rag against it, but neither moved. His head was still bent down toward his work, but had cocked slightly forward. He asked, "Out of gas?"

"Nope. Said the lights worked and everything. The engine just stopped and wouldn't turn over. I called Marcus and asked, he said it started up fine when they went back to tow it the next day."

His head cocked more in Edward's direction. "No cell coverage?"

"That is what he said. He remembered walking past Walter's Creek, and that was it. Nothing for a few days, until he woke up at home," Edward reported. Before Father Murray could ask another question or make a comment, Edward added, "Oh, and get this. Said It was dark and quiet. No sounds of animals, crickets, or anything."

"There are frogs in that creek. I can hear them over my car when I drive by with my windows open," said Father Murray. The chalice was now on the ground in front of him. The rag was a ball of cloth loosely dropped inside it. The base had a nice clear shine, but the rest of it was still dull and dirty. The wooden chair he sat in groaned as he leaned forward and stood up. He walked past Edward and down the center aisle, without saying a word.

"Father?", Edward asked, confused.

"Come on. I will explain on the way."

Edward followed behind and exited the church as Father Murray closed the driver's side door of his Cadillac. Edward took his familiar position in the passenger seat and, as was common, the car was in motion before his door was closed. His seat belt finally clicked closed just before the tires transitioned off the gravel driveway to the tarmac of the road that ran along the front of the church.

"Father, do you mind telling me where we are going?"

Father Murray leaned down and looked out of the windshield to the sky, then said, "We have a bit of daylight left. We need to pick up Lewis first, and then go check those woods. Earlier today, Rick Stenson, Tom Meville, and Fred Tillman stopped by. Rick promised me a few catfish the next time they were out fishing, and had forgotten to bring them by. He made up for it by bringing a plate of his latest catch, already fried up. But before they stopped by, they were out bow hunting up and down Walter's Creek. They didn't bag anything while out. No game, that is, but came back with some really wild stories. The animals they ran into, raccoons, possums, and even the foxes, didn't run away from them. They followed them."

"Followed?"

"Yeah, followed. Tom said he kept looking behind them and saw the same group following them everywhere they went in the woods, and even back to their truck. They never left the tree line, but appeared to stand there and watch them. But that isn't even the strangest. Not by a long shot. Mind you, these are small animals. A fox is no bigger than a medium-sized dog, at best. They aren't aggressive toward humans, or shouldn't be. If memory serves me, some of those are natural predators to each other. They could have cared less about that, though; they wanted the men.

Before they finally pulled off, Rick walked toward the trees to try to scare them all off. He took just three steps before he said each of the animals growled, hissed, and showed their teeth. They never left the woods, but stood their ground. Then, here is where it gets weird. The woods themselves growled and hissed at them."

"Wait. Wait. Wait. The woods, Father? What do you mean, the woods?" stammered Edward, while his body jerked around to face the driver.

"You heard me. He said it sounded like every animal in the woods, all growling at the same time. Now, you and I both know that is not possible, or shouldn't be possible. Just like we've known 99 times out of 100, those animals do everything they can to get away from us, and they most definitely do not follow us."

He was right, and Edward knew it. Considering the strange events lately, he couldn't put anything out of the realm of possibility. One possibility he was hoping for was something a little less odd, and more common. A day out hunting usually involved the consumption of more than adequate levels of alcoholic drinks. Usually of the brown ale variety. He could only hope this trip was no different, and the three men had had a bit too much, maybe even been dipping into someone's homemade shine, and that, combined with their imagination, had got the better of them.

The large white Cadillac slid to a stop in front of Lewis Tillingsly's place. It was a simple log cabin with a wraparound front porch that had two rocking chairs positioned on the longer side of the porch. A sizable place that was deceptive when you looked at it from the outside. Its square shape gave the impression it was small and cramped, but the open concept and light color scheme inside gave it a grand feel. His property was a majestic piece of rolling landscape that had been in the family for over 150 years. An old tobacco farm until the fifties when Lewis' father took to law enforcement and pulled the family out of the agricultural profession. Since he retired, Lewis had toyed around with the idea of returning it to a tobacco farm.

Edward sat still while the car's old springs groaned at the exit of Father Murray. It was the age of the springs, and not the girth of Father Murray, that produced the protest. He disappeared inside, without even appearing to knock on the screen door before going in. The windows were open, and the coolness of a fall afternoon was setting in. A constant symphony of bird calls floated on the pleasant breeze. The gentle rustle of leaves in the trees provided the percussion line under the birds.

Father Murray emerged after a few moments. Lewis Tillingsly was in tow, behind him. They got in the car, the father in the driver's seat and Lewis in the back. He slid in from the driver's side and then to the center of the backseat, then leaned forward, patting Edward on the back.

"So, what grand adventure are we off on now?", he asked.

"He didn't tell you?"

"Nah, just said he needed me to come with him."

"You often get in cars with no idea why or where you are going?", Edward asked, tongue in cheek.

"Yeah, you would think I would know better. So where to, Father?"

"Need to go check out some woods. Edward, tell him what Kevin told you."

Even though there wasn't much to tell, Edward did what he was told. The former sheriff had his law enforcement ears on and asked a few questions. Each of which Edward had asked Kevin, but he didn't have any answer for. After Edward was done, Father Murray recounted the tale the three hunters told him earlier in the day. It appeared to pique his interest, just as it had Edward's. As he explained, a hunter himself, he had had many encounters with animals out in the woods. Those woods, in particular. The animals always scurried away.

"Could they be rabid?", Lewis asked.

"All of them?", retorted Father Murray.

"Good point."

It was a twelve minute drive to Walter's Creek. Father Murray parked on the side of the road, just past the bridge, and the three men got out and carefully descended the embankment to the creek's edge. They walked along the northern edge of the creek. The current setting didn't match how Kevin had described it. There was another hour left of daylight. The silence he mentioned was full of the babbling water and the first hint of night crickets chirping their heads off in the long shadows of the fall afternoon. Every so often, Edward checked his phone and, so far he hadn't lost the signal. They turned into the woods along the old logging road Tom said they had followed. The crumpled silver beer can lay in the grass confirmed their path.

Still no loss of signal. The whole time Edward had three bars or more and, beyond that, he still had a data connection, as confirmed by the social media alerts that vibrated in his pocket every few minutes. That usually dropped first in dead zones.

"How far are we from the squirrels?", Edward asked.

Lewis looked through the woods, off to his left. "You know, not sure. Not too far, if I had to guess. Same side of the road and creek. It wasn't that much further down the road." His eyes continued to look through the woods, and then he pointed to the left, ahead of them. "It is probably that direction. I don't imagine we're past it yet."

A shiver went through Edward's body from just being close to that spot. "I guess the ball field is that way, "Edward said, and pointed ahead of them toward the north.

Lewis agreed, "Yep."

"It's no coinc..." started Edward, but Lewis let out a loud "SHHHH!" that stopped all three of them in their tracks.

"Do you hear that?"

Edward didn't have to ask what the "that" was he referred to, he did. There was something off in the woods, walking along with them. It was small. Not a person. It had four legs. Whatever it was took a few more steps after they stopped, before stopping as well. The woods were deep and thick, providing the animal great cover to stay hidden. Lewis took three steps forward, and the animal mirrored his movements. He moved toward the woods, but this time the response was not footsteps. It was a large growl from, not one, but several, animals. Some were small, but one of them was sizable, formidable, and sent Lewis and Edward stepping backward.

"That sounded like a bear," said Lewis.

Or that was what Edward thought he heard. It was hard to for him to hear anything. He heard the growl. Then a vibration, low at first, but it ramped up quickly to a full on buzz that blocked out all sounds and distorted his vision. His legs were unsteady. Either the ground was moving with the buzz, or his body was.

Lewis took another step backward and joined Edward and Father Murray. When he did, the animals emerged from their cover for the first time. A fox, two coyotes, and a small black bear cub. They moved in unison. All moved forward, but kept their distance at the same time. They were warning, not attacking. Teeth bared. A low growl came from each animal. Their heads were down low, and parallel to the ground, eyes locked on the three men. It was a warning two of the men heeded and stepped backward. Edward couldn't process what he saw. The buzz distorted it. The buzz separated him from the here and now, and locked him in a world of confusion. He felt the hand on his shoulder pulling him a step backward, but didn't know if he took the step or why. The world around him had a layer of static over every sense. No sound. No sight. No smell. No touch.

Father Murray and Lewis pulled Edward back up the logging road. Both walked backward, to keep an eye on their escorts. The creatures followed them, teeth bared the whole time, and producing a cacophony of hisses, growls, and howls. Edward's steps were clumsy at first, but became more deliberate the closer they got to the creek. The static cleared for Edward, just enough to see the creatures following them. When he took a few steps on his own, Father Murray and Lewis let go of him.

Lewis warned him, "Don't run. Move slowly and deliberate."

Edward's hands jerked up to give the universal symbol for "hold up". The creatures were not aware of that symbol and continued to follow.

They continued back up the creek toward the car, and the creatures followed as far as the edge of the woods. From the sound of it, others had joined them. The hissing was deafening. The intent was clear. It was a warning to stay out of the woods. Then, the sound increased beyond a level that Edward thought was possible. The tall pines along the edge of the road bent over them in a threatening posture, and a massive gust of foul-smelling wind sent all three men tumbling to the ground and against the side of the caddy. Edward heard the warning, loud and clear, and scrambled to his feet. All three entered the car, which quickly departed. Figuring out what was warning them would have to take place somewhere else.

19

The mood among the three men sitting stunned in a white Cadillac outside of Lewis Tillingsly's home matched the darkness that had settled in. A layer of fog formed where the remaining heat of the day met the coolness of the night. The air was still. So were the men. Cricket's chirped, but the birds were silent. As were the men.

Edward had been out of the static for a while now, but his head still felt scrambled. His senses dulled. This was like the buzz he had felt just over a week ago, but much worse. Then he was just disoriented. This time, it cut him off from the outside world, and it appeared to be just him. In one of the few exchanges between the longtime friends, neither Lewis nor the father had heard the buzz or seen the static. Only the growling and hissing. Neither sound cracked through the static. To Edward, that told him all he needed to know. This was paranormal in nature, not natural.

Lewis broke the silence and said, baffled, "We need to talk to Marcus."

Father Murray nodded his agreement.

"He is the sheriff. He needs to know," said Lewis.

"Agreed," said Father Murray, and started the car and took off, sending Lewis sliding back in his seat.

"Now?", asked Lewis with a bit of surprise. His breath still taken away by the sudden acceleration.

"Absolutely," Father Murray said decisively.

20

The three men pulled into the parking lot of the Miller's Crossing police department. Father Murray maneuvered into the first open spot and slammed to a stop. When they got out, Lewis stopped and looked at the parking job and then exclaimed, "Father?" The old white-haired priest had a one track mind and continued on to the front door, ignoring the critique of his driving skills. Edward and Lewis followed. The wheels of the Cadillac straddled the lines of two parking spots behind them.

Marcus was standing in the back, past the reception desk, leaning over his desk, with the phone planted to his ear. His speech was fast, agitated. He slammed the phone down and headed toward the three visitors that stood at the countertop used by the receptionist to separate the waiting area from the offices.

"Gentlemen, this is the wrong time for a social call," he sniped from halfway back.

"This is no social call Marcus," said Lewis. "This is official business."

"There's a lot of that going on right now. Hang here. I will send Tony up to take a report." He pushed the button on the countertop to release the door and pushed through the door. With fast, large, determined steps he walked right by them.

"I am afraid that won't do Sheriff."

"And why is that, Father?" he asked as he turned around, perturbed and annoyed. They were keeping him from something. Edward could tell. That matter would just have to wait. Edward couldn't think of much in the criminal history of Miller's Crossing over the last six years that rose to this level. The 'that dog just squatted on my yard', or a dispute over who can claim the carcass if two hunters shot the same game was some of the usual fair. Maybe a car crash or two, but those were usually handled by drivers, with a simple handshake and setting of a date to come over to one another's helping repair the damages. Drunk and disorderlies were the most common calls, and the easiest to deal with. Just had to make sure they were some place they couldn't hurt themselves or someone else. That might mean the lockup for the night, or just a ride home to sleep it off.

"There is something odd in the woods out by Walter's Creek. Animals are working together to keep us out. It is the same area they found Kevin Stierers. It is all related."

"No crap, Father. There is something strange. Fred Moultry was just brought into County General, all torn up. He and his brother were out hunting in those woods, when something attacked him. Laurence said they were separated but he could hear his screams. Now I gotta get over there. You can come along, if you want."

When they arrived and walked in, the six-foot-four-inch frame of a man, who had spent his life throwing hay bails around, manhandling cattle, and raising barns and fences, all by hand, looked small as he sat bent over with his head in his hands. Around him, a flurry of nurses and doctors ran in and out of the room. Amid the sound of orders and responses given in the care of their patient, an occasional moan or scream of pain escaped out the door. Each caused the large callused hands of the figure sitting out front to grip and squeeze the hair on his head as hard as he could, each knuckle turned white with strain.

"Laurence, how is he doing?", asked the sheriff.

Without looking up, he responded, his voice shaken, "Not sure, they won't tell me anything. I just hear what is going on, and it doesn't sound... good."

"Let me see what I can find out."

"Thanks, Marcus."

Lewis took a seat next to the man on the bench. "Hey, Laurence, can you tell us what happened?"

The man tilted his head, tears streamed down his face. "Lewis, I don't know. We were out bow hunting. He thought he heard something move and went off to track it. He wasn't gone more than a minute before I heard the first scream. I ran. He was screaming, over and over, and I needed to get to him. A coyote jumped in front of me, growling and snarling. I tried to go around it, but it snapped at me. I had to shoot it with my bow, twice, to get by. When I found Fred, he was covered in blood. Another coyote and a small bear cub were ripping at his arms and dragging him away. I yelled and charged both animals, but they didn't let go or move. Strangest thing, Lewis." The man stopped his story, and took notice of the others gathered around him. "I have never seen animals act like that. Only after I put my last three arrows through them did they stop."

Edward knelt down on one knee before the man and asked, "What did the coyote and cub look like?"

"Small black bear cub. I would guess only a few months old. Its mother had to be around, somewhere. The coyote, about the size of a medium-sized dog. Grey, with black spots."

"With a white streak on top of its head?", Edward asked.

"Yes. Yes. How did you know?"

"Lucky guess," Edward said, standing up and looking at the others.

Lewis slapped Laurence on the back and said, "I am sure he will be fine. Fred is a tough guy. Going to take more than a couple animals to take him down."

"Laurence, why don't we say a prayer for your brother?"

"I would like that, Father."

Lewis got up and gave Father Murray his seat. He took Laurence's hands in his own and prayed. Lewis and Edward walked down the hallway to let the father tend to the member of his flock.

"Same coyote and cub," Lewis whispered. Edward agreed and thought at least they were dead now. Then he wondered if that were really true.

Lewis looked over Edward's shoulder, whistled a piercing whistle, and motioned for Marcus to join them. He held up a finger and leaned down to tell Laurence something. Dread was plastered all over his face as he walked down the hall toward them.

"How is he?", asked Lewis.

"I have never seen anything like that. They tore him up something horrible. There are internal organs outside of his body. They aren't sure he is going to make it."

Both men shook their heads. The brothers, like most of those in the Crossing, were the latest generation of a family that went back to the beginning. They still lived on the same family farm their ancestors had settled on. Separate houses now, mind you. Each with their own lives, wives, and children. Living on opposite sides of the property, but managing the family farm together. Everyone knew them, not just of them.

"Laurence told us what happened. It was the same cub and coyote we saw."

"Wait... what do you mean?", asked Marcus. His head shook as if he were trying to clear a fog from his thoughts.

At the end of the story, and with the details Laurence had told Lewis added to the end, Marcus stated factually, "Rabid, that has got to be it."

"No, Marcus, it is not that," interrupted Edward. "That doesn't explain why they herded us back and followed us." Just then, it hit Edward like a lightning bolt of rational clarity. "I think they are protecting something. Protecting something out there in the woods."

"Oh, come on, Edward. What would they protect and... how the hell would animals know what to protect?", Marcus asked. Disbelief dripped from every word like cold maple syrup.

"Someone is controlling them. That satanic display we found. That would explain that buzzing that I feel when I am in that area that no one else does."

"Have you ever seen ghosts control animals?"

Edward fired back, "No, but demons can."

"Edward. I respect you and your family. We all do. But not everything that happens here is supernatural in origin. Now, I need to go talk to Laurence." Marcus made eye contact with Edward and Lewis, before he turned and returned to the victim's brother. Edward knew the eye contact was to ensure they knew he meant respect and appreciation, but it was also to drive home the fact that he didn't buy into any other explanation, outside of what was practical. Even though, around these parts, the practical sometimes included what others would consider impractical.

"I am right. I know I am," Edward said harshly under his breath. He leaned back against the wall. Jaw and fists both clenched.

"Edward, I know you are," said Lewis. "Deep down, he does too. He just doesn't want it to be that. He probably remembers how it was before you returned."

"I keep hearing people refer to those as the dark days. What happened back then?"

"Well, your father did a great job of keeping things at bay. Our spiritual visitors were shown the door quickly, and he dispatched the occasional demon to where it came from or ran it out of town where it didn't harm anyone. After his death, there was no one that could do it. Ghosts ran around scaring the crap out of everyone and really creating havoc with the farm animals. That was a bigger deal than you can imagine. Spooked cows produce sour milk. Chickens don't lay eggs. That drove Father Murray to take up the cause. He, like your family, could sense them, but never really got the hang of things. He did well enough with the simple cases. Demons, on the other hand." Lewis joined Edward, leaning against the wall halfway down the hallway from the room where Fred Moultrie moaned and writhed in pain. "Let me ask you this. How big of a murder problem do you think we have here in Miller's Crossing?"

"I didn't know we had one," responded Edward.

"Technically, we don't, but the 37 unsolved homicides and missing persons would say differently. I categorized each of them as missing and, with the help of others, concocted stories about them running off to escape the town, or something to that effect, to keep the state cops off my ass. Some of them we found remains for. Others, we never did. Some did things to hurt themselves, but some of them. God, Edward. I have seen things done to the human body I didn't know could be done. The town helps keep all this hushed, but they all know. They knew Father Murray and I were doing the best we could. It's not like anyone in town could tell anyone the truth. Who on the outside would believe them if they did?"

"Grab the crash cart!" exclaimed a nurse running out of the room down the hall. Laurence and Father Murray both sprang up from their seats as they watched doctors and nurses rush into the room where his brother laid. Father Murray rushed into the room after the flood of doctors. Laurence attempted to follow, but the father performed one last act of comfort before he entered. He turned toward the concerned brother, placed both hands over his heart, and shook his head, then disappeared into the room. The grieving brother was left standing there.

Screams and moans could be heard among the exclamations of medical professionals verbalizing orders and providing statuses. Fred was fading. In both the statuses yelled in the room, and the veracity of his outburst, you could tell. As his screams subsided. So did the orders. There were a few last-minute screams of "clear" from the medical staff. Each followed by a thunderous thud. Each thud produced anguished sobs from his brother. The moans and screams ceased.

Lewis and Edward waited outside the emergency entrance of County General, trying to stay out of the way. Father Murray stayed inside to console Laurence and the rest of the family. Edward looked on as Lewis greeted Fred's wife, hugged her, and said kind words to her. He found it hard to even look at her and her small kids, knowing how their lives had just changed, and the grief they felt. Possibly an open emotional wound from his parent's and Karen's death. Perhaps one that would never close, but some handled it better. Lewis' even-keeled approach to everything probably was the crutch that helped him in matters such as these.

Edward had tried to call Sarah several times on her cell phone, to let her know he would be home late. She never answered. He tried the boutique, only to find out she went home ill a few hours ago. With the subsequent attempts to her cell phone still unanswered, he finally called home, where Jacob answered. Sarah wasn't there, either. He told Jacob that he would be home late and was out with Lewis and the father. A message that was more common than Edward would have liked. As he hung up, Father Murray emerged out the door.

"How is everyone Father?", Lewis asked.

"As good as you can expect. Wendy is pretty shaken up. I will stay a while longer with the family. One of you can drive my car back. Marcus can drive me back to the church later."

"Of course, Father."

"He also is rounding up all the local hunters at the church, 9 AM tomorrow. He wants to go out and find those rabid animals that did this."

21

"Father! Not another word."

Father Murray held back the fire he felt burning inside. Ever since leaving the hospital he tried to explain to the sheriff that there was another explanation for what was going on. Something other than rabid animals. Each attempt resulted in a similar response, with increasing furor.

"Not everything is supernatural. Be rational, Father!"

Being rational is what Father Murray believed he was doing. His rational world included both the natural and supernatural. Could it be rabid animals? Someone who didn't know any better would believe so, or just think the animals were being aggressive. There was one problem. The sheriff didn't experience what Father Murray, Lewis, and Edward did. He didn't watch the animals working together. Working with precision to herd them back. Away from something, but from what? That was the question. That was the question that made Father Murray continue his pleadings with the young sheriff. It was not about being right. It was about protecting his flock. If a group of them stumbled upon "the what", who knew what the animals or "the what" could do to them.

"I am going with you," Father Murray stated plainly, confidently, resolute.

"Father, I said be reasonable. You are not a hunter. You would only be in the way, or a liability. I need expert trackers and hunters. We can handle this."

Father Murray considered himself an expert at tracking and hunting, just not in the arena the sheriff meant. The sport of walking through the woods, swamps, and fields toting a bow or a rifle over his shoulder, in search of an animal whose horns or antlers would be mounted on his wall, was not appealing to him. He wasn't against it. Hearing others talk about it, he could see why they might be interested. It just wasn't for him. Sitting for hours in a boat, with a line in the water. Never seeing the prey you are trying to lure in. Blindly yanking on the hook. All may make fishing seem less than invigorating to others, but it was his passion. To each his own. His feelings didn't make him shy away from enjoying the fruit of those who partake in the sport. Deer jerky ranked right up there next to a nice filet of bass baking under a dollop of butter and herbs in his book.

"Nonsense. I will be fine. I will bring Lewis along. He knows what he is doing. Does that make you feel any better?"

"I guess," said Sheriff Thompson, reluctantly. "You still aren't giving up on your supernatural theory on this, are you?"

"My boy. I have been alive a great many years. What I have seen and experienced has taught me to never discount any possibility, no matter how strange it may appear on the surface. I would be more surprised if it were something as simple as a rabid fox, but I would be relieved. It would serve you well to adopt a similar attitude around this place. It might make your job easier."

"Father, with all due respect. Don't lecture me about how to do my job," sniped back Sheriff Thompson.

"I am sorry. I would never attempt to do that. I meant no disrespect," acquiesced Father Murray. "but I assume you saw the claw marks on Fred's body. They were in sets of three. Much like young Kevin's."

The silence was thick uncomfortable. Only the throaty growl of the 4.6 liter V-8 of the sheriff's Crown Victoria interceptor spoke, and it spoke volumes. Father Murray's comment had produced an impulsive depression of the accelerator that caused the modified transmission to jump into a passing gear. Unnecessary on the vacant country roads. It spoke loudly for a quarter of a mile until the pressure on the pedal was released. Sending that voice into silence.

"The bear probably only made contact with three of its claws. That is all."

"On each swipe? Now, I am no animal expert, but even that seems improbable to me."

The sheriff took his left hand off the wheel and rubbed his brow before smoothing his hair back. What he saw today, aged him several years. Violence in this town was not something he had witnessed often. His predecessor had had that responsibility. Because of the nature of it, he kept it all within. Father Murray knew the look on his face. It was one he had seen on his predecessor several times. The look told of the scene of what had happened to Fred Moultry's mangled body, lying there on the gurney in the emergency room. The blood-soaked sheets around him. Every breath, scream, and moan, followed by a gurgle as blood seeped in from any one of the many mortal wounds made to his body by the huge claws of what ever did this. The sight of the man's eyes searching for help, aid, that will never arrive. The realization that his life was ending. It's a look that sticks with you. Father Murray has given last rites more times than he can remember, but every night he closes his eyes, he sees theirs looking up at him as they realize this is the end.

Some go in peace. Some go with a last word. Fred went somewhere in between. Just after the last moan, there was a single muttered phrase. Father Murray had moved to the bed, to hold the man's hand and pray. To guide his soul home. He was there, but out of the way of those still trying to save his physical form. A skill he had learned over the years. A skill that included reading the lips of a dying person. The phrase that escaped Fred's moving lips was nothing more than puffs of air. To the untrained person, they may consider this as the final exhale, but Father Murray knew it was more. He knew the word the lips said, "Floating".

They pulled up to the church, and Father Murray opened the door. "It's possible, Father."

"What is, my son?", asked Father Henry, his back to the sheriff as he exited the car.

"The bear could have missed with the other claws, or it could have been another animal. There are others out there. Rest assured, we will find it."

"Oh, I have no doubts you will. That is what I am afraid of," Father Murray shut the door, turned, and looked in through the open passenger window. "See you at 9, Sheriff."

22

"It's just a headache," Sarah said.

"I can call Doc Robinson. I am sure he would come out. He does owe me a few favors."

"No dad. Just a headache."

Edward, heard what his daughter said, but his eyes told him more. First, there was the fact she was here. Wild horses couldn't pull her away from Myrtle's for more than just a few minutes. More than once, he had to go down there and force her to go home because she was running a high fever and never should have gone in. More worrisome was her appearance. Her hair was a tangled mess. The curls and body she had added in at Ruthie's a week earlier had already fallen out leaving her naturally dead straight hair, which she straightened every morning before she headed out. What Edward saw now, looked like a brush hadn't run through it in weeks, not just hours. There was also an ashy complexion to her skin tone that made her appear to be an unhealthy gray. Even her lips, instead of the healthy pink they always were, they looked like something out of a black and white movie. She was also in bed, covered by every sheet and blank she had, with all the lights and television off. Sarah had slept with the television on, just with the volume down, for as long as he could remember. "I think it is more, and it worries me," he insisted.

She rolled over against the wall. "It's just a headache," her muffled voice said. "I haven't been sleeping well. Work has been busy. Worried about Kevin and what happened to him, and the entire town has stopped into Myrtle's to ask my opinion about everything going on. It is just exhausting dad."

Everything she said, he understood well. His nerves felt well-worn themselves, and his sleep had been more restless than normal since the encounter with the hum. The events that had occurred since only added to it. It was plausible, but the father in him said there was more. She didn't look well, and there was that parental nagging in his head. "I get that, but I really wish you would let me call the doctor to just check. It would make me feel better."

An angry, but half muffled, moan emerged from his daughter's form. She pulled the covers up tight to her neck and rolled further toward the wall, burying the rest of her face into the pillow. This was a routine Edward had seen before, but she was fourteen the last time. Sarah went through a time when she didn't want to go to school and faked being sick. She would rollover and bury her face in the pillow and pull the covers up as high as she could as a shield against his gaze. He could only surmise that her theory was, if he didn't see her he couldn't force her to get up and go to go school. It didn't work, well not entirely. The first few times, he forced her to get up and go to school. After a while, he realized he missed a key detail in what caused all this. It coincided with Karen starting her first bouts of chemotherapy. One day, he finally gave up and let her stay home. When he came home from work, he found his daughter curled in the bed with her mom. She was holding her mom's head, stroking her hair. It was then it all made sense. Edward let her get away with it a few more times. "Sarah?"

She pushed up away from the pillow a few inches and proposed, "Tell you what. Let me get some sleep tonight, and IF, "she emphasized the word like any great attorney making an argument in front of a jury, "I am not feeling any better in the morning I will let that old Doctor friend of yours come over."

"I don't know," he responded, not quite ready to push his immediate concern aside.

She sighed and turned over to face her father. Her eyes were still closed, when she suggested, "touch my forehead. I am not running a fever."

The low profile bed she had meant he had to lean down, which required him to brace himself with his right hand on her headboard. The palm of his left hand was placed lightly on her forehead. She was correct, no fever. Instead she was icy to the touch. "Sarah, you are freezing," he gasped.

"I know. It's cold outside, and I got chilled, why do you think I am under all these covers?", she said and rolled back over toward the wall, and once again pulled the covers up over her. "Just let me sleep. I will be fine in the morning."

"I don't know, honey," he said. His mind worried, but without evidence of a fever, he couldn't put his finger on it.

"Dad, I promise. If I'm not better in the morning, then I will see the doctor, okay?"

"Okay," he agreed reluctantly. "Let me know if you need anything."

"I will. Will you check the heat?"

"Yep," he agreed.

Edward pulled her bedroom door closed and then turned to the thermostat on the opposite wall. The screen read, 64. That explained the chill he felt when he entered the house. It also explained why Sarah felt so cold, and was covered up so much. He reached up and turned it to 68, and smiled when he heard the system click on.

23

"Did you try to talk him out of this foolishness?"

"What do you think?" Father Murray answered Edward with a perturbed look on his face. "He wasn't hearing none of it. He had thoughts of grandeur in his head. Lead a big posse out. Kill those animals and save the day. Oh, he would be a legend around these parts. The biggest fool that ever wore a badge."

Edward had seen the father frustrated in the past. Edward, himself, had been the cause many times, but never to this level. He huffed as he rattled, agitated, around the church. Picking up hymnals and putting them back in their place. Another huff, before moving on to the next book still sitting on the pew. His mission, which Edward assisted with, was to have it clean and orderly before the sheriff and his men arrived.

"Make sure you don't put two books together. One book for every slot. It's big enough for two, but that means the person on the end won't have one. One book per slot."

"Yes, Father," Edward said, as he slid his twentieth book into the wooden frame hanging on the backside of the pew in front of them. He wasn't sure who would try to put two in there. You would have to squeeze and cram them together to make them fit, even if it were possible, but it must be. Why else would he have reminded him?

The main door at the back of the church cracked open, and a voice boomed in, "Come on in boys." Sheriff Marcus Thompson strutted in, his chest puffed out, showing off the badge that looked to Edward as if it had been polished overnight. "Morning Father," he said as he continued to the front. Behind him was the who's who of the hunters in the region. All dressed in the preferred weekend hunting attire. A sea of red and black flannel, green or camo pants, orange vests, and hats, flooded in. Their old muddy boots thudding on the aged wood floor. The flood continued and flowed into the first five rows of pews. Sheriff Thompson was positioned at the front, ready to tend to his flock. That drew a look and the ire of Father Murray, who stood two pews from the back.

One member of the hunting party hung back at the door, taking in the sight. He stepped forward and leaned over the back of the last row of pews, saying to Edward, "Ever see a larger gathering of yahoos?"

Edward cut his eyes up to the front and then back to Lewis, "Looks like they are after the rascally wabbit."

Lewis had to work to hold back his laughter.

Edward gave Lewis a once over and said, "You look like you kind of fit in."

"Just here for the father. You know what I think this is."

"Yep."

"I bet Marcus spent half the night making phone calls to rally these troops. I am shocked they didn't come walking in lock-stepping like some damn army. At least they left their guns outside."

The sheriff coughed rather loudly from the front and asked, "Shall we begin?" His gaze was on the three men still wandering around in the back of the church. Father Murray stopped his 'cleanliness is next to godliness' work and put the hymnal book he had in his hand in the slot before heading up to the front. Several blue-covered books would have to wait in their spots on the pews until later.

"Okay boys. You all know why we are here. There is a pack of rabid animals out by Walter's Creek. They attacked Kevin Stierers. Messed him up real bad. Then, just yesterday, they attacked and took Fred from us. God rest his soul." Sheriff Thompson paused, crossed himself, and then looked back over his shoulder at the large cross on the back wall above the altar. From where Edward stood, he could almost see Father Murray's body recoil at the display.

He continued, "Well, I say no more. We will go out there and find those animals and kill them before they can harm anyone else. It is up to us to protect our community. Now, from what Laurence told me, there are two coyotes, a bear, and a fox, moving in a pack. That should be easy to find. One coyote is grey, with a white streak on top of its head."

"It would look real good stuffed in my cabin," said a man from three rows back. A few men patted him on the back. Marcus pointed at him and smiled. "That he might, but please don't take any chances. If you see any animals that act aggressive, you know what to do. We have lost enough as it is. Are there any questions?"

"When we going?", asked another man in the front.

"Soon," Marcus said. His hands were folded behind him as he rocked back and forth a little on his heels. Each rock forward thrust his chest out that much further, to show who was in charge. "When we get out there, we will go in the woods together and stay spaced out. Safety is my number one concern today."

"*Right*," Edward thought. This was grandstanding. He knew it. Lewis knew it. Marcus knew it, and planned it. Why? Edward wasn't sure. Perhaps he saw an opportunity to exercise his authority, and show everyone he was in control. A chance to break out from behind Lewis's shadow. Maybe even that of Father Murray, and even Edward, to some extent. Most of the problems in Miller's Crossing were not the type that were dealt with by law enforcement.

"Father, would you like to say a few words?"

Father Murray looked stunned at the request. Edward felt stunned too.

"Maybe a blessing for our safety?", suggested Sheriff Thompson.

The priest shook off the stunned feeling and stammered as he walked to the front of the gathering, "Oh... Okay...Heavenly father. I ask that you watch over these men as they head out into the wilderness. Provide your divine guidance as they search for the creatures that have terrorized our community for the last several weeks. Keep them safe as they do your work, and bring an end to the terror. In the name of our Lord, Jesus Christ, Amen."

"Thank you, Father."

Father Murray brushed him off with a wave of his hand.

"Father, is something wrong?", Marcus asked.

"Eh, ... no. It's nothing," he responded, turning to walk back to the back and resume his task.

"Father, what is it? Something is bothering you," Lloyd Wilcox asked from the second row.

Edward watched as the town's priest turned around, out of respect and love for the members of his flock. The look on his face was still very reluctant when he looked at the sheriff.

"Father, if you have something to say, please, by all means, say it."

Father Murray sighed, and with slumped shoulders, walked toward the first row of pews. The men trained their eyes on him, just as they were during his services, when he took his spot in the center to give a sermon. As he spoke, his body and voice sounded defeated. "Men, I know what the sheriff told you is out there. I think he is wrong."

There was a murmur in the gathering, as the men looked back and forth at each other and whispered among themselves.

"Now, I mean no disrespect," he continued, with a look at the sheriff. "Edward, myself, and Lewis were out there just yesterday. Those animals are not acting like that because of rabies, or any other mysterious disease. Their actions are not natural."

The murmur grew to a louder buzz that consumed the building.

"Now," he continued, louder than before, using his hands to hush the crowd. "Now, something is out there, and it is dangerous. Very dangerous. Rabid animals are sick. These animals were acting together, protecting something. I saw it with my own eyes. They worked together, like you or I would, if we were trying to move someone away. This isn't just a fox or two, protecting a den. This was different species of animals working together in concert. That was not natural. It's anything but. I am worried that one or more of you will stumble into what, or whoever, they are protecting, and suffer a fate similar to Fred. I plead and implore that you don't go."

"Father!" the sheriff interrupted. "That is enough of that. I expected more of you, than to use fear. I sat and talked with Laurence. What he described were rabid animals, not some ghost or spectral being. Perhaps so much time spent chasing ghosts through the years has clouded your judgement, and you see every threat as some kind of wild ghost tale."

"Sheriff?", Edward asked, as he rushed forward.

"I don't remember asking your opinion."

The harshness of the admonishment came out of left-field, and slapped Edward right across the face. Sheriff Marcus Thompson had always been a friendly man. The type everyone liked, and everyone got along with. Not one of those that let the power of the badge he wore go to his head. At least, not before now. This had every sign of what had happened. This was his search, his battle, and he wasn't about to let anyone interfere. The shock of this change knocked the air out of Edward. He looked back at Lewis while he caught his breath. Lewis held up a hand and shook his head. His message was clear, and it took every ounce of self-control to not say another word.

Father Murray added to his protest, "Sheriff, you are running off on a foolhardy search and you are going to get one or more of these men killed."

"I said, that's enough. Now we need to get started." He adjusted his belt and shirt as one that had been in a scuffle might. No one had touched the sheriff, at least not physically. He pulled a folded map out of his back pocket and held it up for everyone to see. "Men, come on up here and let me assign each of you an area on the grid to search, then we can head out and get to it."

Most of the congregation joined the sheriff, up at the map, but a few men straggled around in the pews and never attempted to step forward. Father Murray headed to the back with Edward and Lewis.

"We've got to stop this!", Edward declared, looking intensely at Lewis.

"It's his show now. We will be out there with them. We just need to find it first," he responded in his normal calm and dulcet tone.

"That is too big of a risk to take Lewis. Someone is going to get themselves killed," said Father Henry. He was watching the gaggle of men at the front.

"Yes, Father, it is a risk. But we have the advantage. We have been close before, and have an idea where to start."

"Can't you speak to him?", Edward asked. He lowered his voice as several of the men filed past and out the back door.

"I would be stepping over the line. Remember, guys, I am just John Q. Public now. The same as you."

Father Murray looked dismayed as he watched men he had known their entire lives file past on their way to what he believed was their deaths. Bringing up the end of the line was Sheriff Thompson, who walked by without even casting the three men a look. The men that stood up, but never went to be assigned a grid, waited until the sheriff was out the door before they'd broken their confab with each other, and walked to the back. Three sets of eyes watched them as they did.

"Father, you coming too?", asked Reginald Moore. The man with a salt and pepper beard that hung down to his belly, covering most all of his face, except a little round portion of his nose and his eyes, was about halfway to the back of the church. Behind him were Ted and Able, his two sons. Both students of Edward's. The sullen expressions on their faces told Edward they didn't share the same level of fascination in their tasks the others that walked past did.

"Yes, Reg, I am."

"Good, then we are coming with you. I have hunted all my life. Seen a rabid fox before. They don't do what you say they do." He planted a mighty slap on Father Murray's back.

The six men walked out and saw the dust trail from the several dozens of cars and trucks that had just left the gravel-covered parking lot. In the distance, the rumble of their engines raced toward Walter's Creek. Waiting for them outside was a large man that never came in.

John Sawyer, sporting overalls, like Edward always saw him in, asked, "Lewis, Father. What do you say we get this thing on the road?"

24

The seven men arrived at Walter's Creek. Lewis pulled across the bridge and then off to the northern shoulder of State Road 192, parking behind a long line of trucks and cars. A mass of people milled around the vehicles, strapping packs, vests, and guns in place. A single person stood facing the woods. Like a great General, about to lead his troops into battle, Sheriff Thompson was in an intense stare-down with the woods. The trees, now in full autumn plumage, with much of it on the ground, didn't waver under the intensity. This was a battle, and he aimed to set the tone right now, before the first boots walked into the woods. They would be victorious, and the town would be safe again.

The men lined up, gear ready, along the road and behind the sheriff. They awaited their orders. All but seven, that was. Lewis, John, Father Murray, Reginald, and his two sons, and Edward followed the same path they had earlier, following the creek until they found the old logging road. Behind them, they could hear some great speech being given, a cheer, and then a great rustling as close to forty men pushed into the low brush-covered woods on a search.

The smaller party reached the logging road and cut in. Father Murray explained to John Sawyer and Reginald what they had seen, and where, the whole way. What Father Murray shared challenged what convictions Reginald's two sons may have possessed. Both fell back further, and moved with reluctance, until their father called them forward, "Don't straggle behind. You will be easy pickings for a bear."

Edward's eyes scanned back and forth quickly, to look for any movement, any sign of an animal, or anything out of the ordinary. At the same time, he stayed mindful to his other senses. They might tell him more than his eyes, if they were right about this. Of course, if the great hum showed up again, he would be useless to them. This was why he wanted Sarah to come along. Having another along would be a great help, but she wasn't feeling good last night. She was still asleep when he left, and decided to leave her be, rather than push her to come with him if she was sick.

"Father, I am not sure if it is these woods, or what you are telling me, but something is giving me the heebie jeebies," said John Sawyer. His head looking back and forth through the woods.

"Me, too," Lewis started to say, but was interrupted when he, and the rest of his party, was startled by three raccoons sprinting out of the woods, across the logging road, and back into the woods on the other side. None of the animals broke stride. None of the animals looked in their direction.

"Was that them?", Able asked. The youngest of the two boys' voice sounded fearful and hesitant, just short of a quiver.

There was a pause before any of the men answered.

"No, not likely. With all that noise and racket back there, Marcus's search party is probably chasing anything alive this way."

They were not being covert, not by any definition of the word. Edward could hear screaming and yelling back and forth, between the various groups. Not to mention the constant rustling as they walked on the leaf-covered ground.

Further down the logging road, Edward started to feel disoriented and lost. He stopped, which prompted the others to stop. He closed his eyes tightly and tried to think. Where was he? In the woods. Okay, that was good, he knew where he was, but why was he here? That answer escaped him. The further he tried to chase the answer, the more random thoughts streamed into his mind at high speed. None stayed long enough for him to enjoy or understand. Just something to take up dead space in his head. He was aware enough to know that, but not able to control it. He opened his eyes to look around his surroundings, and saw the group of men standing there around him, silent. Seeing them didn't answer any questions, instead, it gave him more to ponder. Which, when he tried, the hum started, and the static appeared in his vision.

Edward tried to take several deep breaths, to clear both from his senses. That didn't work. His hands rubbed at his eyes, but the static was so dense, he never saw them. Covering his ears didn't block the hum, it intensified it. The more he fought to gain control, the deeper he fell. His whole body, and soul, vibrated. He was not in the world anymore. He was not anywhere. Trapped in a vague, blank, existence; blocked from any external stimulus by the vibrations that he now felt in his teeth. There was pressure on his body, but from what, he wasn't sure. It roamed around his physical form. Pushing. Probing. Then, it stopped and left him there, with only the vibrations and nothing else.

Edward called out, but his voice didn't pierce through the vibrations. He attempted to raise his arms, but he felt them remain limp at his sides. His feet were no longer on the ground. There was no sensation of floating, not that he would know what that really felt like, having never bungee jumped or skydived. There was nothing under his feet. Nothing to press against. No way to run or jump. A twist of his upper body, to try to roll one way or the other, produced no movement at all. Where was he? Who was he?

That was a new question. He couldn't remember who he was. Another question was, what was he? Was he just a thought, or something physical? Something that existed, or just a whimsical thought of someone's, or a dream that will disappear just as fast as it appeared? What is this thing called a dream he had just thought of? The only fact he was sure of, was he was sure of nothing at all.

The static changed from grey to a light green. Why, he didn't have a clue, but found it pleasant. Calming and tranquil. Was that the purpose of the change in color? If so, who changed it? The color pulsed, like waves. Some areas were darker than others, but all were still shades of the same calming green color.

In front of him, a white speck of light appeared in the waves of green. It grew larger and larger and then exploded past and through him. Edward found himself clear of the static, lying on the ground of the logging road. The other six members of their party were all rolling along the ground. Reginald, and his son, Tom, were thrown off the road toward the trees. The trees around them whipped back in recoil, as if blown one way by a horrendously strong gust of wind. The recoil sent them back in the opposite direction, to the point of almost breaking. In Edward's right hand was the cross. Someone had reached into his pants pocket and placed it in his hand. The static and hum were gone. The creaking of a thousand trees and screams had replaced it. The screams were human and coming from the woods. Without hesitation, Edward turned and headed into the woods, toward the screams. Lewis, John, and Father Murray got up, still out of breath from the great force that had pushed them down, and followed. Reginald and his sons hesitated for a moment, before joining the others.

Bushes and branches scratched and scraped at his arms and face as he pushed through, without pause. The sounds of pain were coming from everywhere ahead of him, but he focused on what sounded like the closest group. He pushed through another thicket of brush and into a clearing in time to see a man thrown from the ground, up high against a tree, where his body was crushed and torn to pieces. His arms and legs continued to fly past the tree. What was left of the torso crashed to the ground at its base. Around him, four more men were thrown into the air and suffered the same fate. Others held onto trees they were close to. Their feet dangled in the air. Their arms wrapped around the trunks of the great pines and oaks, holding on with all their might. Mouths gaped open as screams for help escaped. The trees, bent and shook as if they were trying to shake them loose.

A thunderous sound approached Edward from behind. He turned and saw a great wave moving through the trees, pushing them down, parallel to the ground, only to release them and allow them to whip up and back in the other direction as it passed by. Father Murray and John steadied themselves low to the ground as it approached. It thundered like a freight train toward them. Edward held firm where he stood. The ground around him and his friends had a sheen to it. The wave passed by him, and the others that stood close to him, with the gentleness of a spring breeze. All around them, it roared through, sending the treetops down to the ground before letting them go. Men holding onto the trees, lost their grip and were thrown into the air.

Edward watched as some hit trees, pulverizing their flesh into mush. Others flew off into the distance on the wave of air.

Another wave developed behind them. This one appeared larger, stronger, based on the sound and the shake each of the men felt in the ground.

"Let's get out of here!", exclaimed Lewis.

None of the men argued or agreed, they ran and rushed forward through the woods, back toward the road. The wave gained on them from behind. Edward looked back and saw the trees falling to the ground, this time not whipping back up. Everything, as far as he could see, was knocked flat, like dominoes. "Move it!" he yelled, and they all picked up their pace.

Through the trees they saw the road just ahead. Just behind them, trees crashed to the ground as an invisible wave rolled over and pounded the landscape. They ran past Sheriff Thompson, impaled on a branch midway up a tree. A tree that fell to the ground moments after they passed. The four men breached the tree line as the front edge of the wave pushed them, sending them rolling along the ground to the shoulder of the road. It stopped. Behind them was a scene of devastation none of them could have imagined. An entire section of woods, flattened. Trees laid flat on the ground. No sign of the search party. No signs of any life at all, unless Edward looked hard in the distance, where a single grove of trees still stood. It appeared to be the center of the devastation. Trees were laid out away from it, like rays of sunlight projecting from the sun. Surrounding that grove were animals. They encircled it and were facing out, like guards.

Edward, still on his knees on the ground, reached over and tapped Lewis. Lewis was brushing the dirt and grass from his face when he looked up at what Edward was now pointing to.

"What the hell?"

25

Lewis raced back to town as fast as his old '73 Plymouth could go.

They passed people standing outside of their homes, looking in the direction that they just came from. He turned onto State Road 32, Main Street, without pausing at the flashing traffic signals. The tires of the large four-door squealed as they struggled to maintain traction with the tarmac. People flooded the sidewalks on Main Street, standing, looking. Everyone had heard the devastation that occurred in the woods, and they all shared the same confused expression.

"We need to get to the church," Father Murray said determinedly.

Just as determined, Lewis responded, "No. Sorry, Father. We need to get to the police station. I can have someone drive you back." There was no badge on his chest, nor hat on his head, but Edward saw he had transitioned back into Sheriff Lewis Tillingsly.

They pulled into the police station, and rushed to keep up with the long, fast steps Lewis took up the walk and into the building. The normally calm and quiet police station, for this small town, was now a hive of activity. Phones were ringing. Every available deputy was on a phone already. Each had the same frantic look on their face as they tried to calm and reassure the caller on the other end of the line. From the appearance of things, someone needed to calm and reassure them, first.

"Have you seen Marcus?", Wendy Tolliver asked from the dispatch desk. She was the person who normally took the calls and then dispatched one of their four deputies out to it.

Lewis, said stonily, "He's dead."

The buzz in the room ceased. Unanswered phones continued to ring. Voices begged for information from the handsets pressed against the heads of Wendy and the three deputies that were there.

"Tell them you will call them back, and put the phones down," Lewis said, as calmly as he could.

Behind him, Edward was frantically trying to get ahold of Sarah. He needed her help with this. She was not at home, or the boutique. It surprised him to learn from Jacob she left just after he did. It also dismayed him to hear from Jacob that he had heard the rumbles all the way back at their home. Their home was as far from Walter's creek as you could get. He called her cell phone, it rang four times before going to voicemail, sending a vibration of worry through him.

In the distance, the rumbles continued. Like a thunderstorm several counties away. It rolled closer and shook the ground, then stopped. Minutes later, it started again.

"Guys, there is something out there. We don't know what it is. It flattened the woods around Walter's Creek."

"Flattened?" asked Russ Hamilton, a 22-year veteran of the force, eyes wide and mouth agape. A look replicated on the face of the others that stood there listening to Lewis.

"Every tree, and," Lewis swallowed before he continued. Edward watched as he delivered the news, amazed at how the dead-stone concentration in his eyes never wavered. "It killed everyone in the hunting party Marcus took out there. We barely escaped, and I bet Edward's trinket had something to do with that."

Two phone handsets crashed to the desk. Another tumbled out of a hand to the floor, pulling the phone off the desk.

"There is no other way to say it, this has been a devastating day. It's not over, as you can hear." Lewis pointed a finger in the air as another rumble rolled in the distance.

Edward looked around the room. It dripped in fear. Law Enforcement was about catching speeders dragging on Main Street, or kids skipping school. Dealing with the apocalypse was not in their job description. It was a better fit in Edward's job description, if such a thing were written. Even then, he didn't have a clue how to handle this.

Wendy asked, reluctantly, "What do we do, Chief?"

That was the question Edward had no answer to and froze at the realization that Lewis may turn and look to him for advice. He was the "expert" in the room. That moment never arrived. He never turned around to ask Edward, he didn't turn to anyone, flinch, or miss a beat. He made a quick wipe across his thick mustache and steadied himself.

"Our focus is protection. Where is Tony?"

"He was out on patrol," Wendy said.

"Get him on the radio."

Wendy sat down, put the headset on, and keyed up her radio. Her movements were slow and deliberate. She had worked dispatch every day for the last 29 years. A fact she began every embarrassing story with at Lewis's retirement party. Making a call is something that should be second nature, but there was a pause before and after each movement. Almost like she was double checking.

"Tony, you out there?", she called, a crack in her voice.

"Yeah, I am here. Wendy, what the hell is happening? I keep hearing explosions."

Wendy's head dipped and landed in her hands. Her body shook at her desk.

"Wendy?", the voice over the speaker asked.

Lewis walked forward, past the reception desk. Edward could feel a sense of calm and confidence creep into the room and everyone in it. He leaned down to Wendy and said something softly. She took off the headset and leaned back. Tears streamed down her face.

Lewis put the headset on. "Tony, it's Lewis. Where are you?"

"On North Bluff, just past Jackson Hollow," Tony said, sounding surprised to hear his old boss's voice over the radio.

"Okay, I need you to get over to State Road 192, just East of the Walter's Creek bridge. Do not go across or get out of your car. Just tell me what you see. Got it?"

"Uh, yeah, Lewis. On my way," Tony responded.

Lewis walked back and joined Edward, Father Murray, and John, in the small waiting area.

"It will take him a few minutes to get out there. We need to know what is going on out there and keep everyone away. Everyone in town can hear that rumble. It won't be long before spouses, and family members of those that went out there with Marcus, start trying them on their cell phones. With no answer, they will ride out there to check on them."

It was clear to Edward; Lewis was in charge now. He was back in his element.

"Russ, do you know if Marcus had a list of those who volunteered with him this morning?", he asked, looking back at the stunned deputies that were now standing around consoling Wendy.

"N... No. I don't think he did."

"Father, any chance you remember everyone who filed into the church this morning?"

"I think so," Father Murray said, deep in thought. "I will start on a list."

"Put Wendy's husband, Daniel, on the list."

Father Murray walked up to the reception area, where there was a sign-in sheet and a local Fraternal Order of Police mug full of pens. He set to work on the list.

"Now what?", Lewis whispered to John and Edward.

"I don't know. I am trying to get ahold of Sarah. She can help."

Lewis nodded.

"Once the father has the list put together, do we need to start notifying people?" asked John.

Lewis nodded again, and then added, "At some point. I need to know what is happening out there. Hearing those rumbles continue has me concerned. There is no one out there for whatever to attack or force out."

A sick feeling landed in the pit of Edward's stomach. He understood what Lewis's concern was. They had left, and everyone else was dead. Why was it continuing? Was the area of devastation growing? His knees felt weak, and he needed to move before he fell right there. With his cell phone in hand, he walked out in front of the station. A click of the redial on his phone produced the same result. Four rings, and then her voicemail picked up. A call to the boutique went unanswered. Which was less worrisome. When they sped through town, everyone was outside looking. Another call, and Jacob answered. "Hey Jacob, have you heard from Sarah yet?"

"No. I tried her cell and texted her. Nothing," replied Jacob. "Dad, what's going on? The whole house is shaking." Edward hadn't heard his son's voice like this before. Not even when Karen had died.

"I don't know, Jacob. Just keep trying your sister and stay inside."

"Okay, Dad. I'm scared."

"Me, too, sport. Me, too."

26

The radio rattled to life and words fired out of it at the speed of machine-gun bullets, "Wendy! Wendy! Wendy! What the hell is this? What the hell is all this? It's all gone. Gone. Nothing."

"Calm down Tony," Lewis said. "Just breathe and tell me what you see."

"I can't describe it so you will believe, not what I am seeing. No way."

"Some of us will. We were out there when it happened. Now tell me what you see," Lewis told him. Keeping his voice calm and soothing. A contrast to the frantic tone of the deputy on the other end.

"The whole forest is laying down on the ground. Flat. From about a hundred feet south of 192, and a little further than that, across Walter's Creek heading ea..." a huge roar over the radio cut it off. When it subsided, Tony screamed, his voice several octaves higher than his usual tone. "What the fuck was that? I needed to move back. It threw my patrol car in the air and another row of trees just fell."

"Tony, pull back as far as you can while still keeping eyes on it. Understand?"

"Yes, I understand, Lewis. Am I happy about it? No, but I understand."

"Lewis," Edward called.

With the headset on, Lewis walked out to the waiting area. Edward had attempted to call Sarah several more times, to no avail. His gripped his cell phone tightly in his hand, to avoid missing any returned call or message from his daughter. As Lewis came closer, Edward shared the one concerning detail he had pulled from Tony's screaming and swearing, "It grew."

The comment appeared to hit a bell of clarity in Lewis. He snapped his fingers and rushed back closer to the radio, asking questions the whole way. "Tony, can you hear me?"

"Yeah?"

"You said another row of trees fell. Where?", he asked.

"Right next to me, and in front of me. Was afraid the damn things would fall on me, but they fell straight out."

"Tony, where were they in relation to the highway and creek?", Lewis asked, looking at Edward.

"A row or two east of the creek, and south of the road."

Lewis pressed the mute button on the headset and whispered, "Shit," and rushed to the reception desk. He fished in the various drawers for a few seconds and then yanked out a large map that he rolled out on the countertop. Edward ran to meet him. This thing grew with every rumble. Which were all at regular intervals of 1 every ten minutes or so. It wasn't breaking any speed records, but not slowing or coming to a stop.

Edward put the question of the mysterious force, and what the causes were, out of his mind and studied the map from that spot out. The map was a street-level view, based on a satellite photograph from high above. The streets and community of their small, peaceful town were clearly visible. Each house represented a resident, a family, a friend. Each wanted their slice of happy Americana. Each now lived in the middle of a nightmare. His hands immediately pointed out spot after spot on the map. Most of which Lewis appeared to have already noted with his eyes, as he motioned for Russ to come over to the desk. The spots Edward pointed out were the first homes in danger, if this continued. With no sign it was stopping, he had to assume it wouldn't. Science and math were never his strong suit and at the moment he was only guessing, but a guess was better than nothing. That guess estimated maybe two hours before it reached the first house. A house that undoubtedly contained an occupant or occupants that were scared to death. With its proximity to the source, everything in the house had to shake and rattle with every rolling wave of whatever it was. If they had not already fled, they would need to be moved to safety.

"Russ, I need you to get out to Kyle's place. Get him and Mildred out and bring them to the high school. With her health, he may try to put up a fight, but don't let him. Tell him I said so, okay?"

Russ said nothing. Just nodded and put on his brown wide-brimmed hat. He rushed past them and out the front door as Edward shifted their attention to the next spot he pointed out. A single road, with approximately 20 houses on it. They were next. His finger circled them, and Lewis said, "Yep."

He turned around slowly and looked back at the crying, wilted, woman that had been his dispatch officer for the better part of 29 years. A sigh escaped his lips before he said, "Wendy? I need you, are you okay?"

Her face was red with grief and streaked with makeup. Okay was a feeling Edward didn't think she would feel now, or anytime soon, but he watched her hands make frivolous attempts to wipe away the tears. A slight jerk up straightened her position. "Lewis, what do you need?", she asked. Her voice still quivered, but had a sense of resolve and strength.

"Get on over to the high school. Call Rob Stephens on the way and have him open the gym. We will use that as a shelter, for now. At least until we can get a handle on this," his eyes looked at Edward as he said the last statement.

"Good idea," was all she said as she stood up and went on her way.

Then Lewis turned back to the men standing on the other side of the counter. He stood up straight and, if he wore his old utility belt with a gun and cuffs attached on it, Edward would imagine this would be one of the times he hitched it up. "John. I need to deputize you. You up to it?"

"Just say the word," he replied, without hesitation.

"I need you and Terrence back there to head out to Riley's Ridge and go door-to-door. Instruct them to head to the high school. They're probably frightened, so be gentle."

"Got it," John said. "Terrence, you're with me. Let's go."

There was no hesitation by the deputy. He was up and past them, heading out the door before John could turn around and take a step.

"John?"

"Yeah, Lewis?"

"Don't dent him. He's new," Lewis responded, with as much of a wry smile as any of them could manage at the moment.

"Lewis, why don't we go with them? We can cover more ground," suggested Reginald. His two sons stood blankly behind them.

He agreed, "Good idea. Get them out of there as soon as they can, and regroup at the high school."

There were just three men left standing in the police department, with phones ringing off the hook behind them. Edward studied the map and located the next area they would need to move to get to safety. Each time he started a new search, his eyes went back to the same spot. That area on the map where a single grove of trees stood among all the devastation.

"Lewis, how can we help?", asked Father Murray.

"Well, Father. You two can figure out a way to stop it."

Both men looked at each other, and then the ground beneath their feet. Edward hoped for divine intervention as he turned his cell phone over in his hand and pled for the screen to show an incoming call or message. Then he asked for divine intervention to give him some kind of idea of what to do. Both prayers went answered. All he knew for sure was, he had to go back out there to learn more, but he didn't have any intention of going alone.

"I need Sarah. She has more training and is stronger than I am."

"She still not answering?", Lewis asked.

"No."

"Then let's go find her," he said, grabbed a walkie from the charger, walking around the counter and heading toward the door.

Edward looked back at the ringing phones, and the lack of anyone else back there to field the calls, or man the station. "What about the phones?"

"Nothing we can tell them will make anyone feel better."

Before Edward exited, he took one final look back. Phones rang. The extension lights on the old-fashioned plastic green phones flashed. No one was left to man the station. Something Lewis would never allow to happen while he was Sheriff. It was a matter of standard operating procedure. These were times that were anything but standard.

27

Back up Main Street they sped, or as much over the limit Lewis dared to go. His car didn't have lights or appeared official, in any capacity. The lack of cars on the road made it unnecessary. It bounced over the bumpy country roads. A few of the bounces had a little something extra in it as another wave of the mystery force rolled in. Shortly after the bounce, the portable radio Lewis grabbed squawked to life. Tony reported seeing another line of trees falling down in a large heap, sending up a cloud of dust. He had backed up a quarter mile down the road and parked at the apex of a curve, still giving him a full view of the events unfolding. Still too far for his liking, something he commented on several times over the radio, but the furthest he could go and still see.

Lewis, Edward, and Father Murray pulled into a diagonal spot in front of Myrtle's. A crowd had gathered on the sidewalk outside of each and every store. Everyone looked in the direction of the rumbling. Mouths hung open. A few attempted to cover them with their hand. The boutique was no different. Judy Spencer stood just outside the door, facing the common direction, with the same expression as the rest of the masses, plastered on her face. Edward got out of the passenger side door of Lewis's Plymouth and headed for the door. As he passed Judy he asked, "Sarah inside?"

"Uh huh," said the distracted teenager. Edward opened the door causing the little bell to ding. The simple sound seemed to snap Judy out of her trance. "Oh, no. Sorry. She is not here. She opened up early and then left."

Edward let the door close and asked Judy, "Where did she go?"

"She didn't say. Have you tried her cell?"

"Yes," he said frantically. "Several times. She hasn't answered."

He turned to Father Murray and Lewis, who were standing at the edge of the curb, next to the large green beast they had arrived in. "She isn't here," he said, with his hands out to his sides, exacerbated.

"Where would she be?", Father Murray asked.

Edward thought. Her not being at the store made little sense. That store was her life, her passion, her responsibility. She would never leave it alone. Not unless it was an emergency. He knew of only one, maybe two, other times she had left Judy alone, in charge of the store. Once, when she was sick, and the other was just recently. Then it hit him, and he turned back toward Judy, almost sprinting.

"Judy, do you know where Kevin lives?"

Judy thought. Her hand moved from in front of her mouth to her chin. "Yes. Yes, I do. His family lives in the brown house on Cattail Drive."

"Do you know the house number?", he asked anxiously. The ground under their feet rumbled again. A few moans escaped the gathered crowd.

"No, sorry. Sarah and I rode out there one day after we closed, to drop something off. It's the only one of that color. Just take a right off of Main. Pretty easy to find."

Edward turned and ran back to the car. He was in the passenger side before either of the other two men even opened their doors. The driver's side door opened and, without being asked, he said, "Cattail Drive."

"Good, it's close," said Lewis.

It was just two cross streets past the end of the main shopping district. A single light that hung from a cable across the road. It blinked yellow in the direction they were coming from, and red to the cross-traffic. On either side were lines of trees, like most of Miller's Crossing. No houses were visible when Lewis took the right.

"Lewis, you there?", Wendy called over the radio. He picked up the radio with one hand, while expertly turning the car with the other. "I'm here."

"People are arriving at the high school. Rob and a few other teachers have set up cots on the Gym floor."

"That's great Wendy. Nice work. Keep them as comfortable as you can."

"Will do. How many evacuees do you think we need to prepare to handle?"

Now that was a question that no one in the car knew the answer to, but Lewis didn't let the lack of an answer hang there and cause any feeling of uncertainty creep in for those in his charge. "Let's prepare for the thirty families. That should cover the areas we identified earlier. We will adjust, if needed."

"Will do."

"Keep up the good work, Wendy, and thank Rob and those other teachers for me," Lewis said. The radio dropped to the seat beside him.

A half mile down the road, the first house came into view. It was white, with black shutters. Another stretch of trees and another white house. On the opposite side of the road, surprise, another white house. Edward started questioning if the local hardware store sold any other colors. Then, it came into view. A brown two-story house, no shutters, with a matching attached garage. Nothing special, but nothing too simple.

"There!", he exclaimed.

"I see it," said Lewis as he whipped the car into the driveway and gave the brakes a stomp. His car slid to a stop, sending the occupants jostling back and forth inside.

The ground rumbled under them again. Edward got out and shut the door as the radio came alive again with Tony's latest report. He didn't wait to hear. He didn't need to. They all felt and heard the ground rumble. There was no ignoring it. The shrillness in Tony's voice just added to the terror that hung over them all. Like when the killer drags the knife across the metal pipe in the basement, just to torment his victim for a few seconds longer.

Edward mounted the steps and banged on the door. He didn't pause to see if anyone heard and was coming to the door, and kept banging the whole time. The hinges were loose on the metal screen door, allowing the door to reverberate and sound like a large cymbal crash every time he hit it. With every unanswered knock, the speed of his knocks increased. One bled into another, until it was one big noise of vibrating and banging metal, that never paused.

The large windowless wood door behind it clicked and opened. A woman in a tattered terry-cloth robe, and worse attitude, cracked the door open. Her eyes were as welcoming as a tarantula, and glassy. Her voice had the warmth of the arctic circle when she asked, "Can I help you?"

Edward didn't care about her attitude, or lack of welcoming demeanor. The location of his daughter was his focus. "Is Sarah here?"

"What?", she asked discourteously.

With his agitation at an all-time high, Edward snapped, "Sarah Meyer, my daughter. She is dating your son, Kevin."

The woman straightened herself. The scowl curled up, in both the mouth and eyes, in an attempt at a smile, which still lacked any sense of warmth. A hand reached up and attempted to comb through her hair. A finger caught a tangle and jerked it out with haste. "So, you are the ghost guy, huh? I haven't seen you around, yet. Cuter than I thought."

The ground rumbled under his feet again. Mrs. Stierers took notice and grabbed the door frame firmly with both hands and squealed, "What the fudge was that?"

"Mrs. Stierers. I really need to find my daughter. It's urgent."

"Ummm. Yeah," she stammered. Her eyes looking past Edward at the world around them. Searching for the source of the rumble and loud noise that shook her out of the hangover she suffered, from whatever she had enjoyed too much of last night.

"Sarah!", Edward shouted through the open door.

"Knock that off," she demanded. "She ain't here. Left here early this morning with my boy."

"Do you know where they were going?", Edward asked eagerly.

"Nope."

Edward threw his hands up and walked down the three steps, back toward the car.

"What the hell is going on?", she asked. Her voice shook. It was either fear, or the hangover sneaking back in.

"Don't know, Mrs. Stierers. Go back inside and stay safe," Lewis said, standing outside the car, next to the open driver's side door.

Her eyes darted in his direction. A hand jerked up above her eyes to shield them from the midday sun. "Sheriff?"

Edward yanked the car door open and got back in. It slammed behind him with a metallic rattle. Any ability to soften the sound had long left the thirty-year-old gaskets. Lewis followed, and the car rocked side to side as both men settled in.

"She isn't here. Said her and Kevin left earlier, and has no clue where they went," Edward said. There was a tone of defeat in his voice, and the air went out of the car.

"Now what?", Father Murray asked as Lewis backed out of the driveway and pulled off.

Edward looked down at his hands in his lap. His mind was blank, but his body was in motion. At some point after he entered the car, his hand reached into the pocket and fished out the familiar cross and book. The fingers of his right hand traced the edges of the cross. What used to be square edges were now rounded and worn, from centuries of being handled. The stem more worn than the crossbar. The dark, aged wood still had evidence of stains, from what, Edward didn't know. The feeling of it was familiar. The size, the shape of it, was comforting. It was more than physical. That old piece of wood stirred something deep inside of him. Clarity. Focus. It had from day one.

"I need to go back out there. I have to face it," Edward said sternly, decisively.

28

"You're nuts," Tony said over the radio, from his post a quarter-mile away.

Inside, Edward had to agree, but that didn't change the fact that he was sitting in the passenger seat of Lewis's Plymouth, driving out to Tony's position, to walk in there and confront the mysterious force. Nothing in his core felt fear. To feel fear, he would have to know what was out there to be afraid of. Fear of the unknown was not in his nature.

"Guys?"

Lewis answered the radio call from John Sawyer, "Yes, John. Go ahead."

"We just left the last home. Everyone is clear. Terrence will drop me off there with Tony. I am going in with you."

Edward snatched the radio out of Lewis's hand. He flipped it around several times, looking for the button to push to talk, like he had seen in many movies and television shows. There wasn't just one button, there were several. Lewis grabbed it back, and with one hand spun it around and pressed the button on the top left. The static that came through the speaker cut out for a second and then returned when he released the button. Then he handed it back to Edward. All without taking his eyes off the road.

"Absolutely not, John!", Edward exclaimed. His hands shook as he waited for a reply, but one never arrived.

"Father, talk him out of this," Edward turned to the back seat and said. His hand offered the radio to Father Murray, but he never took it. Just shook his head, and mouthed, "You will need the help."

Edward turned back around and let the radio fall to the seat in frustration. It bounced twice, before landing on the floorboard. Lewis never looked down at it, but his facial expression showed his displeasure. Edward leaned forward to retrieve it and watched Lewis's expression as he put it back on the seat. The frown disappeared.

The rumbling continued, still at the same intervals as it had for the last hour, but the intensity picked up the closer they got to the area. When they pulled up next to Tony's cruiser and got out, the intensity of each crash was so strong, each of them had to bend their knees to avoid falling over as the earth quaked below them. A cloud of dust rose from the area, creating an odd unnatural haze that resembled a battlefield under heavy bombardment. The only thing missing was the smell. Instead of the smell of gunpowder, or anything burning, there was a very sweet and almost pleasant pine smell in the air, from the thousands of cracked and mangled trees. It was natural, not like one of those hanging air fresheners.

Terrence's cruiser pulled up behind them and John got out and joined the others standing in front of Tony's vehicle. Terrence stayed standing behind his open door. Hands firmly planted on the door frame, and eyes taking in the scene in front of him.

The earth shook below them, again. Both cruisers, and Lewis's Plymouth, bounced on their springs. The seven men were sent staggering as the trees a few yards ahead of them fell flat, sending up a huge plume of dirt, adding to the haze.

Edward took a few tentative steps forward. The steps grew more confident. Held firmly in his hand was the old familiar cross. Father Murray followed him. John and Lewis fell in behind, with rifles over each of their shoulders.

Edward heard a twig snap behind him and turned. His heart sank as he saw his friends following him. "Stay here," he insisted. "This is too dangerous. I don't know if I can protect you."

"Nonsense. Who will protect you?", said Lewis. His hand tapped the butt of the rifle hanging over his left shoulder.

"I can't let you," Edward started to say, but John interrupted him. His voice gruff and deadpan. "Edward, we know what we are getting into. We were doing this with Father Murray before you arrived, and your father before him. This is our town, our home. Now, let's go take care of this."

Edward turned around and walked, with his friends following. He held the cross out a little further in front of him. It had protected them before, he hoped it would do the same as they walked back in. The ground around him had a yellow hue to it, which gave him a little confidence.

The path in was not as easy to walk as it was when they had entered that morning, or when they had escaped. There wasn't a clear piece of ground anywhere. They walked up and over destroyed and pulverized tree after tree. Some were just cracked trunks and limbs. Others were nothing more than sections of sawdust.

Each wave of air passed by harmlessly around them. It whipped tornados of dirt, dust, and small branches everywhere, sending them crashing back to the ground, but none of it came within six feet of the men. A cocoon of faith protected them, and Edward was at the point. The bubble didn't protect them from the shaking ground, which made each step as they traversed the downed trees treacherous.

Their target, the grove of trees, grew larger on the horizon with every step. It was a small patch of forest, maybe twenty trees wide, among the landscape of destruction. When the wind exploded out toward them, those trees in the grove didn't move. In there, it was a calm fall day. Figures moved around the edges of it. It was the animals. In particular, the fox and the wolves. Arrows, stuck out of each of them. They paced back and forth, equally distant from each other.

John Sawyer took the rifle from his right shoulder and raised it to sight in on the animals. "I can take them from here. Lewis?"

Lewis pulled the rifle from his left and did the same. "Yeah, I can, too."

"I got the wolf on the left."

Lewis, then called out, "I got right."

Both men shot. Both shots hit, dropping the wolves right there. The fox in the center didn't run off at the crack of gunshots that echoed across the flat land. It stood still until a third crack brought it down. Both men shouldered their rifles, and the party continued forward. The sulphur smell of gunpowder mixed with the sweetness of pine in the air.

As they approached the grove, another group of figures appeared. At first they moved in and out of the trees, just at the edge, hiding from view, but showed enough to be seen. Then they stepped out of the shadows, into the sun.

"Father, will bullets work against those things?", John asked. A cocked rifle was already up and pressed firmly against his shoulder.

"I don't know, John," answered Father Murray.

Those things, as John called it, were grunting, seething, and spitting creatures that were not of this world. Each the size of a very large dog, but that was where the comparisons ended. They were green, and covered in tumorous skin. Large ears adorned their pointy snouted heads. Most of the time, they were down on all four long legs, that ended in feet with long claws, but it was obvious they were just as comfortable on two when they reared up and screamed. The sound was not one Edward had heard before. It was nothing like any of the ghosts, or the few demons he had encountered. This was more primal.

Two shots rang out from either side of Edward. The shots struck two of the three creatures, but did not drop them. The bullets hit their targets, forcing both to recoil back at the impact, but that was it.

Another volley hit both square in the chest mid-scream. Again, they just shook it off. Edward heard a rustling beside him as both Lewis and John reloaded. The creatures took the pause as an opportunity and rushed at them. There was less than twenty yards separating them from the creatures.

"Hurry!", Father Murray said.

The rustling on either side of him continued, but faster. Edward looked to his side as he heard the click of Lewis loading a shot in his rifle and sliding the bolt back into the place. John had just fished a bullet out of his pocket. A blast came from Lewis's rifle, striking one creature in its brawny shoulder, causing it to stumble, but after just a few steps it shook the impact off and continued. John fired and hit the third one for the first time. The shot hit its elbow, or knee, on the front left leg, sending it down to the ground. It got back up and rumbled along with a limp.

It wasn't working. They were only ten feet away when Edward bent his head and said a silent prayer, while holding the cross out in front of his chest in two outstretched arms. The yellow hue that surrounded them on the ground grew deeper and expanded out. Edward continued to pray. Father Murray joined him. A bright white light projected from the cross, forward, hitting all three beasts, freezing them mid-stride where they were. They hung in the air.

"Try now," Edward said. His voice calm and resolute. Two volleys exploded from either side of him, ripping into the creatures. Another hit the third. All three fell limp in the air. Edward lowered the cross, and they fell into large heaps on the ground.

Edward walked around them. The smell of them was a combination of rot, blood, and a stench he had never smelled before. Lewis poked at one with his rifle. Edward watched for any movement, but there was nothing.

29

The four men stood at the edge of the grove and peered in from the outside. Even without foliage, the tall pines and oaks generated shadows. A gentle breeze above them caused those shadows to dance, creating the illusion of creatures moving around among the trees. Outside of the creaking of the swaying trees, and the crackling of leaves under their footsteps, the area was dead silent. No scurrying of animals. No rustling of leaves.

The woods were dense, forcing the men to weave in and around the trees. It also blocked their view to not much more than a few feet in front of them. With each step, they looked. Both Lewis and John held a loaded rifle at the ready. Each had a second one loaded and slung over their other shoulder. Edward lead the way, holding the cross out. Hoping it would continue to protect them, while fully expecting to be charged by another creature, with every step. The earth outside the grove rumbled again, and they heard it, but didn't feel it. Inside the grove was not affected. No quake beneath them, and no gust of wind. The trees that towered above them continued to sway in the light breeze, but that was all.

A haze formed in front of Edward. First just above ground level, and barely obscuring his vision, but as they moved in further it became denser, until it blocked his view of the ground around their feet, and it felt thick as he stepped through it. His legs felt numb at first, then he picked up the sensation of a vibration running up them.

"Are you guys seeing this?", Father Murray stuttered.

"Okay, good, someone else is seeing the fog. I was wondering if this was that static again," responded Edward.

"Edward, look up."

Edward took his focus off the dense fog that was getting denser, and the strengthening vibrations, and looked up as John asked. He was not prepared for what his eyes saw, and what he was about to come face to face with. Like the display they ran into before, there were desecrated animal corpses hanging there in the air, but this time, there were no ropes or strings that Edward could see. The headless deer, with its front legs cut off, hung there at eye level. Blood dripped down and pooled on the ground. Several feet away, another headless deer spun around slowly in the breeze.

Slowly, Edward stepped around the animal's body. Each step more uncomfortable than the previous, but his eyes stayed up, ignoring the fog. They ran into several other animal corpses hanging in the air. All headless. Some were missing their front legs. Some were missing their back legs. The intestines dangled from a few. The air took on the putrid odor of death.

"What's that?", Father Murray asked.

Edward stepped back behind a tree and watched for a charging beast, but none came. He looked around, but there was nothing.

"I see it, Father. Not sure," Lewis said. "Maybe an old hunter's shed."

"That's what it looks like to me," agreed John, and he and Lewis moved forward to check it out.

Edward looked again, but he saw nothing. Just a few trees right in front of him. A dense cloud of fog cloaked everything else. "Where is it?", he asked.

"Right in front of you," Father Murray said.

"Where?", he asked again.

"Edward, it is about ten feet in front of you, and to your right. It is pretty big, you can't miss it," said Lewis.

"I can't see anything through this fog," he said.

"What fog?", Father Murray gasped.

"You don't see this fog?"

Edward heard rustling leaves around him and then felt a hand grab the hand that held the cross and raised it higher. The immediate space around the cross cleared, allowing him to see a dirty and dilapidated shed, with a flat roof and aged wood panels, with various layers of peeling paint. The side that faced him had a four-paned window in it, each cracked or shattered. He stepped forward to investigate. A low bush stood between him and the shed, and he shifted the cross from his right hand to his left hand, to free up his right to push the bush out of the way. When he let go of the cross for the split second it took to transfer it from one hand to the other, he was thrown back into the void he had experienced before. Surrounded by a gray static that nulled each of his senses. It lasted for only a second or less, but was disorienting, all the same. When the cross touched his left hand, he was pulled back into the present and he knew what the fog was. It was the static, it was trying to consume him again, but the cross was negating it, somewhat.

When his vision cleared, he saw the window of the shed. Inside, a light flickered from side to side like the flame of a candle. The window was too high for him to see in. He pressed his ear to the wall and heard something. He wasn't sure what it was, but it wasn't nothing. There was a noise inside. "Someone is in there, I can see a light," he said urgently. "Find the door. We need to get in."

Edward ran along the wall and rounded the corner when Lewis and John found the door on the front. It was a simple, wood plank door, with a diagonal board across it for support. Large, black, iron hinges connected it to the doorframe. A single brass knob stuck out from the door, without an accompanying lock. Father Murray was reaching for the knob when there was a scream from the other side. A shape leapt from the trees at the men. It grabbed John Sawyer around the head as it jumped over them and, in a single move, yanked his head off at the neck and flung it through the woods. John's body fell slack on the ground, with blood spurting. His windpipe wheezed and gurgled as his lungs took their last breaths. The shape disappeared into the woods as fast as it had appeared.

The three men stood there in shock, looking at their dead friend. Then survival instincts set in and they turned their backs to the shed and focused on the woods around them. Edward searched the woods with his eyes and his ears but, once again, they were in complete silence. The trees around them no longer creaked in the breeze. It was still. Unnaturally still. Leaves on the ground around them began to float in the silence. First just a few, but then, all of them. They didn't move, or spin, just floated.

"My God," exclaimed Father Murray. "Fred's last word was floating. I bet he found this place, and ran into whatever that is."

Mixed in with the leaves were pebbles, branches, were shards of glass, that Edward had to assume came from the broken window. He turned, attempted to open the door to the shed. It was locked. He put his shoulder into it, hard, and the old wood planks in the heavy door cracked, but didn't open.

The scream came again, and the shape lunged out at them from the woods again. Lewis leveled the rifle he had at the ready and fired two shots into it. Unlike the creatures they ran into earlier, the shape fell and rolled around in pain. All three men had a good view of Kevin Stierers' bloodied body on the ground. He screamed and snarled with a crazed look, and his hands clawed at the ground. Lewis pulled his second rifle and, without hesitation, fired a third shot, this time right in his head. Putting an end to the screams. His body laid just feet from John's.

Edward tried the door with his shoulder again, but it still held. Lewis pushed him aside and kicked it. His large booted foot landed squarely just above the knob, sending the door exploding inward on its hinges. A gust of air exploded out, sending Lewis flying and crashing into a tree, back first. His limp form fell to the ground at the base of the tree.

Without a second thought, Edward rushed through the door, cross first, and then froze at the sight of his daughter in a seated position, floating above a pentagram drawn in blood. Black candles dotted the points of the pentagram. A chant in another language filled the room, but she was not speaking it. A cold chill resonated through his body, and the world around him vibrated. Edward moved around the pentagram on the floor, his daughter's solid white eyes followed him.

"Sarah!", he yelled.

She did nothing.

"Stop this!", he pleaded.

She held out a single hand, delicately. A single finger attempted to extend itself from the others, to touch him. There was a gentleness to this. A tenderness.

"Sarah!", he yelled again.

Her lips finally parted, and mouthed, "Help me."

A tear traced down Edward's cheek as his heart sank inside his chest. His little girl was in trouble, and he didn't exactly know how to help her, but he had to try.

Her hand turned over, with her palm upward. It reached for him to grasp it and, on instinct, he reached forward.

"Edward, don't!", screamed Father Murray. His warning was heard, but there was no way Edward planned to pay any attention to it. He was going to grab his daughter and yank her out of there, and then go after whatever had her trapped there in midair.

His fingers touched her, and a flash ran through his essence. He saw the bodies of his parents on the kitchen floor. Karen, as she took her last breath. The births of both Jacob and Sarah, and then his own death. Jacob, standing over his casket, mourning his loss. Father Murray, performing the burial rites as he was lowered into a hole next to his parents. Then, as quickly as it had all arrived, it was gone. Darkness replaced everything. It was an all too familiar void. Edward had been there before, which lessened his surprise when that same voice echoed around him, "I told you I would be back."

Outside the void and in the shed, his body flew limp and lifeless against the wall, before collapsing in a pile on the floor. The hand that clutched the cross bounced. On the rebound, the fingers opened, letting the cross slide from his grasp.

30

The constant slow breeze of air coming through the vents carried a sterile smell everywhere as Jacob sat in a chair not meant to be sat in for longer than a few minutes. His aching legs and back, attested to that fact. They had endured a marathon session of thirty-two hours straight, with only a few minutes away to stretch or visit the bathroom. The other chair in the room was more of a lounge chair, or so it seemed. The red vinyl cushioned structure had a tall back and leaned back a little, if you pushed down on the handle. Its occupant, Father Murray, had been there for about as long, minus an hour the day before, when he left to go tend to his concerned parish members who were holed up in the high school gym.

Jacob appreciated him being there. He had no one else. Lewis Tillingsly had spent the majority of his time there, but now had other responsibilities, following the death of Sheriff Marcus Thompson. The small police force had lost its leader and, due to lack of experience, or recent emotional losses, no one besides him was suitable to take that position. It wasn't official. He wouldn't wear a badge or uniform, but that didn't diminish the weight of his words. They would follow him, just as they had for years.

Lost in Marcus's search party were the sheriff, Mayor Chris Chandel, Chamber of Commerce chief Walter Spencer, two council members, and scores of husbands and sons. Forty-three, in total. Normal city operations ceased at that moment. Everything that happened from that point forward was just a reaction to the emergency. Over the next few days, the numbness of the shock would wear off, and grief would set in. Then panic and fear would follow.

The only question in Jacob's mind about the next few days was, would his dad wake up? He laid in the hospital bed that sat between him and Father Murray, with wires running to monitors, and a ventilator to help him breathe. He hadn't regained consciousness since his hand had contacted Sarah in the shed. None of the medical tests the doctors at County General had given him had found anything medically wrong with him, but their capabilities were limited. They were just a small medical center.

Father Murray and Lewis had argued for the better part of an hour the day before, about trying to transfer Edward to one of the larger cities, where the facilities were more modern. It pained Lewis, Jacob could tell the inner conflict he felt, to argue against trying to seek better help for his friend. As protective as he wanted to be of Edward, he had to be the same, or more so, to the town. If they transferred him, there would be questions. How could they explain it?

Out the window behind Jacob, just over seventeen miles away, was the only other family he and Edward had. She sat quietly in a shed, still floating above the ground, or so they believed. No one had laid eyes on her since they left. The progression of the attack had stopped nine hours after Lewis and Father Murray had pulled Edward out. Four square miles of forest were leveled flat. The trees that had once stood so proudly, were pulverized to nothing but dust and twigs. No homes were damaged, it had stopped short of them, but Lewis took a wait and see posture about letting anyone return home. Some wouldn't want to. Feeling the earth jump and shake under their feet was enough to spook them to the point of never wanting to return. Every major incident that happened in Miller's Crossing drove one or two families away. No one could blame them.

"Hey, Jake. How is he doing?", asked a head poking through the door of the hospital room.

"Still the same," Jacob said to Mark Grier.

Mark walked in and stood at the foot of the bed, looking at his friend of a long time. Father Murray was leaned back in the chair to the right, asleep. Mark kept his voice down and said, "Don't you worry. Your father is a tough man. He once broke his arm at the beginning of baseball season, and still made the last two games. How are you doing?"

Jacob looked up at his father's friend, wearily. He was tired. There was no denying that. Father Murray had dozed off a few times in the chair, but Jacob hadn't been so lucky. Not that his body hadn't tried, but his mind had other intentions. Each time his eyes fell heavy, his mind played a picture show of his father and his sister. He knew from what he had heard Lewis and Father Murray talk about that Sarah was at the center of all of this. That was something he couldn't believe, but his mind still constructed images that matched what he had heard the men talk about. It created a war in his thoughts and dreams. Images of her floating, with everything evil his mind could conjure around her. Flames of red, orange, and black everywhere. Then a kind image of her blue eyes looking at him with that same annoyed, but loving, look she always gave him. One image to battle the other. He felt alone, and scared. "I am fine, Mr. Grier."

"How long has he been here?", Mark asked as he pointed to Father Murray.

"Most of the day."

"Good," Mark said. His gaze back on his old childhood friend.

Jacob hadn't taken his eyes off his father, except for a few moments here and there when talking to a doctor, nurse, or other visitor. Every second he hoped to see his eyes open, or a hand move.

Mark backed up and leaned against a cabinet against the wall, and watched. Silence surrounded all three men. The only sound was the silent, but constant, pump in and out of the ventilator, and the occasional snore from Father Murray or the creak of the vinyl in his chair as he shifted.

They all just stood in silence for the better part of an hour before Lewis Tillingsly stopped by to check on Edward. When he walked in, he shook Mark's hand and exchanged a quiet greeting, and then took up his post against the cabinet next to Mark. There was no small talk, or there could have been, and Jacob never noticed. He locked his eyes on his father and didn't look anywhere else. His thoughts were there and everywhere. His state of exhaustion had now allowed the war of thoughts that had only occurred when his eyes closed to now invade his waking thoughts, ripping apart what was left of his emotional sanity. A tear and sniff escaped, but he caught them before they progressed to anything more. There was no concern in his head about anyone else noticing. There wasn't room for anything so insignificant.

"Lewis, you copy?", squawked the radio attached to Lewis' hip.

He pulled it off and stepped toward the door. "Lewis here. What is it Tony?" He stopped just short of the hallway. Far enough to muffle the conversation behind the door, but still close enough for everyone in the room to hear it. The sound rustled Father Murray awake, partially.

Over the radio, Tony reported, "She is out, and walking toward the town. She is not alone."

Ready for what is next for the Meyer's Family?

Dear Reader,

Thank you for taking a chance on this book. I hope you enjoyed it. If you did, I'd be more than grateful if you could leave a review on Amazon (even if it is just a rating and a sentence or two). Every review makes a difference to an author and helps other readers discover the book.

As for what's next for the Meyer's family, you can keep reading with book 3 – The Exorcism of Miller's Crossing. I have included the first chapter below.

As always, thank you for reading,
David

P.S. Signup for my readers list and I'll send you my monthly list of free offerings from other authors and notifications of my new releases: www.authordavidclark.com. You will receive the Miller's Crossing prequel – The Origins of Miller's Crossing – for free, just for joining.

DAVID CLARK

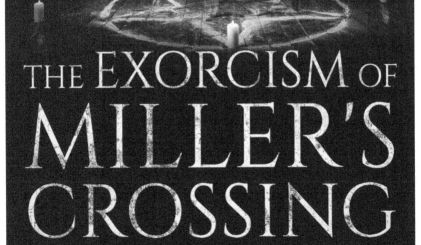

THE EXORCISM OF MILLER'S CROSSING

1

Days turned into a week in Miller's Crossing, but only the calendar recorded the passage of time. The sun continued to come up in the morning and disappeared in the evening, but not even the light of day could crack through the darkness that loomed over the town. This wasn't the darkness of night or a storm cloud, this darkness was heavy and wet. Like the type you find in the furthest and deepest corner of a leaky basement, down where mold, mildew, and the fear of things that *go boo* lived. The difference here, the things that *go boo* were walking the streets.

Its citizens had taken refuge at the high school or their own homes since what they called, "the event." Most only braved a daylight raid out for supplies, but even that was a tentative and dangerous effort. No one moved alone or blindly. They always checked around the corner to make sure nothing was there before going further. Only a few stores remained open. Two days after the event, Ted Barton moved into the back storeroom of his local grocery and mercantile. Every morning he stepped outside and look to see what was around and then re-locked the door; that's the only time he actually goes outside. The rest of the time he stayed in the store, watching and waiting for anyone that may come in need of food or supplies. When the sun started to dip, and shadows stretched across the street and his storefront, he retreated to the safety of his back storeroom. The sound that came from the portable television Ted had kept back there since the Cuban missile crisis was that battled against the screaming and howling outside.

Two days after the event, Lewis Tillingsly closed down the roads into and out of town under the guise of road work. He even went as far as sending a press release to all the neighboring towns to be read on the radio, and to the Lynchburg local news. To further sell the story, he and Frank Micheals took two farm tractors out and dug up large sections in the road, leaving piles of dirt as obstructions. To every outsider, it would look like road repair or bridge replacement. To Lewis, the new sheriff, it was a necessary protection to buy the time they needed to get things under control. How much it would buy him, he didn't know. A few locals used the old grown over logging roads to make an escape, but they knew enough to not tell.

While most of the residents of Miller's Crossing remained in hiding, unless they needed to go out, a few attempted to take a stand once their own fear dissipated. Lewis had used emergency alert programs set up after 9/11 to send a specific order to every member of the town. That message stated, "Do not attempt to confront these creatures. Stay inside." Most heeded it; some did not. They headed out in patrols just after dusk, armed with whatever they had on hand: Everything from hunting rifles, to farming tools, and a few homemade Molotov cocktails. Their goal was the take back their town. Their achievement was adding to the loss of life total.

Jacob could see the fires they set with their attempted attacks burning from the window of his father's hospital room. Edward had not moved or spoken since that day. Every doctor in town took a shot at reviewing his condition. Each left scratching their head, no closer to the cause of his condition or a treatment to bring him around. Jacob had only left a few times during that time; once to take a walk and try to clear his head, which didn't work. There was a constant something there, what he didn't really know. He mentioned it to Father Murray once, who explained it was probably him sensing the ghosts and demons that now roamed openly around town. That was possible. He had felt a few times, but it had come and gone. Now it stayed and never left.

The other time he left his father's side was a move of honorable intent but foolhardy execution. Lewis had just left his father's room after receiving a radio call about another raiding party attempting to confront several demons around Westside park, just under a mile away from the hospital. Jacob heard him order Tony to stop them before he rushed out himself to help intervene. The response from Tony told him that Sarah was with them. To Jacob's knowledge, that was only the second time she had left the shed since all this started. No one had talked to him directly about everything they knew, or had they? He had to hope they knew more about what was going on than they told him, which was nothing. What was clear is she was the key at the center of all this. If he could get through to her, he could put a stop to all this, a thought he considered rather deeply as possibly the last thought his father had before what happened to him.

He ventured out and saw a sight that beat any horror film he watched late on Friday and Saturday nights. Animal-like beasts walked around on two legs, screaming, howling, and snorting. Their claws scratched against the concrete of the sidewalk in an ominous screech. At the center, his sister. Still dressed in what she wore the last time he saw her, but that was all recognized. Her eyes wide and solid white. A cape of raven hair flew around behind her as she floated down the road and up into the park. Her arms and hands directed the creatures without a sound. They maintained a ring around her. One that he couldn't find a way through. He watched as the raiding party rounded the corner, firing their rifles at the creatures. A few rushed at them, swinging axes and machetes. The flails were wild, and only connected a few times, not that it made any difference. They brushed their attacks off like gnats on a summer afternoon.

Lewis's voice echoed through the loudspeaker on top of Tony's cruiser. "Stop and disperse, for your own safety." He repeated it over and over again above the screaming, but it was too late. Those were not from the creatures. They were from the men that attempted to attack them. As a last gasp attempt, they threw a flaming bottle at Sarah. It hit and exploded around her, but not on her. Inside that sphere of flames, her skin changed. Marks and symbols pressed through her skin from the inside while her lips moved. With the single flip of her hand, she sent those flames back at the attacker, Clay Harris. The ball of flame lifted him off the ground and up into the sky, like a shooting star rising from the ground, and disappeared from view. Then, without warning or cause, she disappeared, just as she had the first time she had emerged from the shed. Jacob could only assume she had returned like she had before.

That trip was last night. Lewis saw him and caught up with him halfway back to the hospital. Jacob wasn't running back like he had on his way out. Instead, he was walking, defeated, and exposed. Lewis gathered him in Tony's patrol car. There was no grand lecture on how stupid he was for doing this. Jacob merely sat in the back and cried. When he went out, he knew he wanted to help but didn't know how. Seeing her like that cemented in him how hopeless that situation was. That was no longer his sister. She was something different. Evil. The destroyer of the world she had become part of over the last few years. Her actions killed people she had grown to call friends and family, and didn't even hesitate. Look what she had done to her own father.

When Tony dropped Jacob and Lewis back off at the hospital, they walked in through the emergency room. Each bay around them was full of victims from tonight's encounters, either from the raiding party or those that were caught outside after dark. The fate of the victims was already sealed. That didn't stop the medical staff from continuing to try to save them. This was a nightly occurrence.

Back up in Edward's room, Lewis called in Wendy Tolliver and placed Jacob in her care under "house arrest." Her instructions were to not let Jacob go anywhere, which she hadn't. Every time he shifted in the chair and got up to walk around the room, she took a position at the door. Even when he walked down to take a shower, she walked by his side the whole way like she was escorting a prisoner to lockup. If he had any other plans to leave, it would have to be out the window. Not an option from four stories up.

Click the links below to keep reading "The Exorcism of Miller's Crossing".
For the US Store, tap here.
UK, tap here.
Canada, tap here.
Australia, tap here.
Everywhere else, tap here.

Want more Miller's Crossing? Check out the Miller's Crossing series?

The Ghosts of Miller's Crossing
Amazon US
Amazon UK

Ghosts and demons openly wander around the small town of Miller's Crossing. Over 250 years ago, the Vatican assigned a family to be this town's "keeper" to protect the realm of the living from their "visitors". There is just one problem. Edward Meyer doesn't know that is his family, yet.

Tragedy struck Edward twice. The first robbed him of his childhood and the truth behind who and what he is. The second, cost him his wife, sending him back to Miller's Crossing to start over with his two children.

What he finds when he returns is anything but what he expected. He is thrust into a world that is shocking and mysterious, while also answering and great many questions. With the help of two old friends, he rediscovers who and what he is, but he also discovers another truth, a dark truth. The truth behind the very tragedy that took so much from him. Edward faces a choice. Stay, and take his place in what destiny had planned for him, or run, leaving it and his family's legacy behind.

The Demon of Miller's Crossing
Amazon US
Amazon UK

The people of Miller's Crossing believed the worst of the "Dark Period" they had suffered through was behind them, and life had returned to normal. Or, as normal as life can be in a place where it is normal to see ghosts walking around. What they didn't know was the evil entity that tormented them was merely lying in wait.

After a period of thirty dark years, Miller's Crossing had now enjoyed eight years of peace and calm, allowing the scars of the past to heal. What no one realizes is under the surface the evil entity that caused their pain and suffering is just waiting to rip those wounds open again. Its instrument for destruction will be an unexpected, familiar, and powerful force in the community.

The Exorcism of Miller's Crossing
Amazon US
Amazon UK

The dark days of Miller's Crossing's past, were nothing compared to life as the hostage of evil demon hellbent on revenge.

With Sarah Meyer possessed, Edward Meyer in the hospital, and Jacob Meyer unprepared to battle the evil that has invaded the town, Father Murray reached out for help in the form of the other "keepers" from around the globe. When they arrived, they found Hell on Earth, but were undeterred and rushed into action to save the town and one of their own. They must take action to avoid losing the town, and allowing the world of the dead to roam free to take over the dominion of the living. This demon took Edward's parents from him while he was a child. What will it take now before it is done?

The Haunting of Miller's Crossing
Amazon US
Amazon UK

Some memories are more haunting than the scariest demon,

Jacob has taken the reigns from his father on both the newly opened family farm, and the family's responsibilities around the town. Even though it has been years, the wounds of what his family has gone through, especially in regard to his sister, are still open and very raw. He struggles with moving forward in the world of the living, but excels in dealing with the world of dead. But, the world is about balance. A strong force of good, means somewhere there is an equally strong force of evil just waiting for the perfect time to emerge. The days of simple and harmless ghosts are just stories from Miller's Crossings past. The ones that roam around town now are dangerous, and it is getting worse. Can Jacob do what the keepers couldn't and remove the final trace of the great scar from the town of Miller's Crossing, or will he let that and the bad memories from the past haunt him and future generations to come.

Prequel - The Origins of Miller's Crossing
Amazon US
Amazon UK
There are six known places in the world that are more "paranormal" than anywhere else. The Vatican has taken care to assign "sensitives" and "keepers" to each of those to protect the realm of the living from the realm of the dead. With the colonization of the New World, a seventh location has been found, and time for a new recruit.

William Miller is a simple farmer in the 18th century coastal town of St. Margaret's Hope Scotland. His life is ordinary and mundane, mostly. He does possess one unique skill. He sees ghosts.

A chance discovery of his special ability exposes him to an organization that needs people like him. An offer is made, he can stay an ordinary farmer, or come to the Vatican for training to join a league of "sensitives" and "keepers" to watch over and care for the areas where the realm of the living and the dead interaction. Will he turn it down, or will he accept and prove he has what it takes to become one of the true legends of their order? It is a decision that can't be made lightly, as there is a cost to pay for generations to come.

ALSO BY DAVID CLARK

The Dark Angel Mysteries

The Blood Dahlia (The Dark Angel Mysteries Book #1)

Amazon US

Amazon UK

Meet Lynch, he is a private detective that is a bit of a jerk. Okay, let's face it he is a big jerk who is despised by most, feared by those who cross him, and barely tolerated by those who really know him. He smokes, drinks, cusses, and could care less what anyone else thinks about him, and that is exactly how the metropolis of New Metro needs him as their protector against the supernatural scum that lurk around in the shadows. He is "The Dark Angel."

The year is 2053, and the daughters of the town's well-to-do families are disappearing without a trace. No witnesses. No evidence. No ransom notes. No leads at all until they find a few, dead and drained of all their blood by an unknown, but seemingly unnatural assailant. The only person suited for this investigation is Lynch, a surly ex-cop turned private detective with an on-again-off-again 'its complicated' girlfriend, and a secret. He can't die, he can't feel pain, and he sees the world in a way no one ever should. He sees all that is there, both natural and supernatural. His exploits have earned him the name Dark Angel among those that have crossed him. His only problem, no one told him how to truly use this *ability*. Time is running out for missing girls, and Lynch is the only one who can find and save them. Will he figure out the mystery in time and will he know what to do when he finds them?

Ghost Storm – Available Now

Amazon US

Amazon UK

There is nothing natural about this hurricane. An evil shaman unleashes a super-storm powered by an ancient Amazon spirit to enslave to humanity. Can one man realize what is important in time to protect his family from this danger?

Successful attorney Jim Preston hates living in his late father's shadow. Eager to leave his stress behind and validate his hard work, he takes his family on a lavish Florida vacation. But his plan turns to dust when a malicious shaman summons a hurricane of soul-stealing spirits.

Though his skeptical lawyer mind disbelieves at first, Jim can't ignore the warnings when the violent wraiths forge a path of destruction. But after numerous unsuccessful escape attempts, his only hope of protecting his wife and children is to confront an ancient demonic force head-on... or become its prisoner.

Can Jim prove he's worth more than a fancy house or car and stop a brutal spectral horde from killing everything he holds dear?

Game Master Series

Book One - Game Master – Game On

This fast-paced adrenaline filled series follows Robert Deluiz and his friends behind the veil of 1's and 0's and into the underbelly of the online universe where they are trapped as pawns in a sadistic game show for their very lives. Lose a challenge, and you die a horrible death to the cheers and profit of the viewers. Win them all, and you are changed forever.

Can Robert out play, outsmart, and outlast his friends to survive and be crowned Game Master?

Buy book one, Game Master: Game On and see if you have what it takes to be the Game Master.

Book Two - Game Master – Playing for Keeps

The fast-paced horror for Robert and his new wife, Amy, continue. They think they have the game mastered when new players enter with their own set of rules, and they have no intention of playing fair. Motivated by anger and money, the root of all evil, these individuals devise a plan a for the Robert and his friends to repay them. The price... is their lives.

Game Master Play On is a fast-paced sequel ripped from today's headlines. If you like thriller stories with a touch of realism and a stunning twist that goes back to the origins of the Game Master show itself, then you will love this entry in David Clark's dark web trilogy, Game Master.

Buy book two, Game Master: Playing for Keeps to find out if the SanSquad survives.

Book Three - Game Master – Reboot

With one of their own in danger, Robert and Doug reach out to a few of the games earliest players to mount a rescue. During their efforts, Robert finds himself immersed in a Cold War battle to save their friend. Their adversary... an ex-KGB super spy, now turned arms dealer, who is considered one of the most dangerous men walking the planet. Will the skills Robert has learned playing the game help him in this real world raid? There is no trick CGI or trap doors here, the threats are all real.

Buy book three, Game Master: Reboot to read the thrilling conclusion of the Game Master series.

Highway 666 Series

Book One – Highway 666

A collection of four tales straight from the depths of hell itself. These four tales will take you on a high-speed chase down Highway 666, rip your heart out, burn you in a hell, and then leave you feeling lonely and cold at the end.

Stories Include:

- Highway 666 - The fate of three teenagers hooked into a demonic ride-share.
- Till Death – A new spin on the wedding vows
- Demon Apocalypse - It is the end of days, but not how the Bible described it.
- Eternal Journey - A young girl is forever condemned to her last walk, her journey will never end

Book Two – The Splurge

A collection of short stories that follows one family through a dysfunctional Holiday Season that makes the Griswold's look like a Norman Rockwell painting.

Stories included:

- Trick or Treat – The annual neighborhood Halloween decorating contest is taken a bit too far and elicits some unwilling volunteers.

- Family Dinner – When your immediate family abandons you on Thanksgiving, what do you do? Well, you dig down deep on the family tree.
- The Splurge – This is a "Purge" parody focused around the First Black Friday Sale.
- Christmas Eve Nightmare – The family finds more than a Yule log in the fireplace on Christmas Eve

WHAT DID YOU THINK OF THE DEMON OF MILLER'S CROSSING?

First of all, thank you for purchasing *The Demon of Miller's Crossing*. I know you could have picked any number of books to read, but you picked this book and for that I am extremely grateful.

I hope that it provided you a few moments of enjoyment. If so, it would be really nice if you could share this book with your friends and family by posting to *Facebook* and *Twitter*.

If you enjoyed this book and found some benefit in reading this, I'd like to hear from you and hope that you could take some time to post a review on Amazon. Your feedback and support will help this author to greatly improve his writing craft for future projects and make this book even better.

You can follow this link to *The Demon of Miller's Crossing* now.

ABOUT THE AUTHOR

David Clark is an author of multiple self-published thriller novellas and horror anthologies (amazon genre top 100) and can be found in 3 published horror anthologies. His writing focuses on the thriller and suspense genre with shades toward horror and science fiction. His writing style takes a story based on reality, develops characters the reader can connect with and pull for, and then sends the reader on a roller-coaster journey the best fortune teller could not predict. He feels his job is done if the reader either gasps, makes a verbal reaction out loud, throws the book across the room, or hopefully all three.

You can follow him on social media.
Facebook – https://www.facebook.com/DavidClarkHorror
Twitter – @davidclark6208

Cover designed by Johannes Klein

This book is a work of fiction. Names, characters, places, and incidents either are products of the author's imagination or are used fictitiously. Any resemblance to actual persons, living or dead, events, or locales is entirely coincidental.

David Clark
Visit my website at www.authordavidclark.com

Printed in the United States of America

First Printing: June 2020
Frightening Future Publishing

Made in the USA
Monee, IL
09 August 2022

11296190R00075